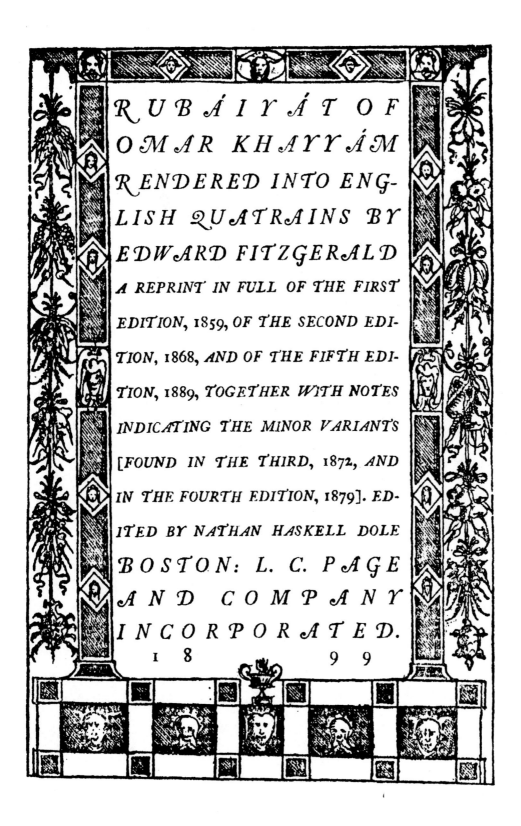

RUBÁIYÁT OF OMAR KHAYYÁM RENDERED INTO ENGLISH QUATRAINS BY EDWARD FITZGERALD

A REPRINT IN FULL OF THE FIRST EDITION, 1859, OF THE SECOND EDITION, 1868, AND OF THE FIFTH EDITION, 1889, TOGETHER WITH NOTES INDICATING THE MINOR VARIANTS [FOUND IN THE THIRD, 1872, AND IN THE FOURTH EDITION, 1879]. EDITED BY NATHAN HASKELL DOLE

BOSTON: L. C. PAGE AND COMPANY INCORPORATED. 1 8 9 9

CONTENTS

Yon rising Moon that looks for us again—
How oft hereafter will she wax and wane;
    How oft hereafter rising look for us
Through this same Garden—and for *one* in vain!

FITZGERALD &

OMAR KHAYYÁM

FITZGERALD AND
OMAR KHAYYÁM

EDWARD *FitzGerald undertook the study of Persian in 1853 when he was about forty-four years of age. He found his first pleasure in it in the charming illustrations from Háfiz, Sádi and other poets cited by Sir William Jones in his "Grammar." In October of that year he bought the Gulistan of Sádi and during the next two years he read with Professor E. B. Cowell at Oxford the "Salámán and Absál" of Jámi, which he translated into verse and published in 1856 and afterwards reprinted as an addendum to the fourth or 1879 edition of his Paraphrase of the "Rubái-yát of Omar Khayyám." That same year Professor Cowell discovered among the MSS. belonging to the Ouseley Collections in the Bodleian Library a beautifully written scroll containing 158 quatrains of the date of 1460. He made a careful copy of it and sent it to FitzGerald, who in turn copied it for Garcin de Tassy in Paris. Garcin de Tassy published a brief article or "Note sur les Rubaï'yat de 'Omar Khaïyam" in the* Journal Asiatique *of 1857 and with slight variations in a pamphlet of the same date. In this he transcribes ten quatrains from the Ouseley MS., giving it implicitly to be understood that he had discovered the MS. But as FitzGerald had asked him not to mention himself or Cowell in that connection, perhaps he was not to blame.*

FitzGerald himself seems to have at first attempted to render Omar into Latin, reproducing the peculiar rime of the rubâ'i and scanning it like a mediæval poem. One of these is preserved in FitzGerald's correspondence and may fairly be reproduced here : —

Tempus est quo Orientis, Aura mundus renovatur,
Quo de fonte pluviali, dulcis Imber reseratur;
   Musi-manus undecumque ramos insuper splendescit,
Jesu-spiritusque salutaris terram pervagatur.

According to his own account he versified a number in the same way.

FitzGerald found greater and greater delight in Omar. In June 1857 *he wrote Professor Cowell : —*

*"By to-morrow I shall have finished my first Phy-
siognomy of Omar, whom I decidedly prefer to any
Persian I have yet seen, unless perhaps Salámán."
About five months later he says:—*

*"And now about old Omar. You talked of sending
a paper about him to* Fraser, *and I told you, if you
did, I would stop it till I had made my comments.
I suppose you have not had time to do what you pro-
posed; or are you overcome with the flood of bad
Latin I poured upon you? Well, don't be surprised
(vexed you won't be) if I solicit* Fraser *for room
for a few quatrains in English verse, with only
such an introduction as you and Sprenger give me
—very short—so as to leave you to say all that is
scholarly, if you will. I hope this is not very cava-
lier of me. But, in truth, I take old Omar rather
more as my property than yours; he and I are
more akin, are we not? You see all [his] Beauty,
but you don't feel with him in some respects as I
do. I think you would almost feel obliged to leave
out the part of Hamlet in representing him to your
audience, for fear of mischief. Now I do not want
to show Hamlet at his maddest; but mad he must*

[11]

be shown, or he is no *Hamlet* at all. G. de Tassy eluded all that was dangerous, and all that was characteristic. I think these free opinions are less dangerous in an old *Mahometan* or an old *Roman* (like *Lucretius*) than when they are returned to by those who have lived on happier food. I don't know what you will say to all this. However, I dare say it won't matter whether I do the paper or not, for I don't believe they will put it in."
FitzGerald's forebodings regarding the rejection of his article on Omar were justified; but it was not because Omar was too Oriental for the magazine. Seventeen years before — in April, 1840 — Fraser had published an anonymous article on Persian Poetry, and among the other poets mentioned was "*Omar Chiam or Khy-Yoorn!*" here also called the "*Voltaire of Persia.*" This article has so far apparently escaped notice from bibliographers, but the execrable doggerel translations by which he is represented in it and a part of the text were taken without credit by Louisa Stuart Costello in "*The Rose Garden of Persia,*" published in 1887. Professor Cowell was now in Calcutta, having ac-

cepted the position of Professor of History at the Presidency College, and as he had just discovered there a lithographed edition of the Rubáiyát containing 492 quatrains, he communicated to the Calcutta Review of January, 1858, a critical article containing metrical, but for the most part unrimed, versions of thirty-one of the quatrains. That same month FitzGerald gave his paper to the editor of Fraser, *but months passed and the magazine did not publish it. In November he wrote to Professor Cowell:* —*

"As to Omar, I hear and see nothing of it in Fraser *yet; and so I suppose they don't want it. I told Parker he might find it rather dangerous among his Divines; he took it, however, and keeps it. I really think I shall take it back; add some stanzas which I kept out for fear of being too strong; print fifty copies and give away; one to you, who won't like it neither. Yet it is most ingeniously tesselated into a sort of Epicurean eclogue in a Persian garden."*

This threat he carried out; in January, 1859, he wrote to Cowell: —*

[13]

"*I took my Omar from* Fraser, *as I saw he did n't care for it; and also I want to enlarge it to near as much again of such matter as he would not dare to put in* Fraser. *If I print it, I shall do the impudence of quoting your account of Omar, and your apology for his free-thinking; it is not wholly my apology, but you introduced him to me, and your excuse extends to that which you have not ventured to quote, and I do. I like your apology extremely also, allowing its point of view. I doubt you will repent of ever having showed me the book. . . .*
My translation has its merit, but it misses a main one in Omar which I will leave you to find out. The Latin versions, if they were corrected into decent Latin, would be very much better."
And again writing in 1861, *he says:—*"*I doubt I have given but a very one-sided version of Omar; but what I do only comes up as a bubble to the surface and breaks.*"*
The "*eclogue*" *which* Fraser *rejected was pub-*

---

* *He calls his translation of the Parliament of Birds* "*no translation, but only the paraphrase of a syllabus of the poem, quite unlike the original in style too.*"

lished with a brief biographical preface and the promised citation from the Cowell article and with a few notes, in a thin paper-bound pamphlet in 1859. The oddness of the title, the silent fame of the author and the fact that no translator's name was on the title-page were reasons sufficient, without considering its pessimistic philosophy, to prevent the little book having any vogue. It did not even keep its modest price but Quaritch, to whom Fitz-Gerald presented the unsold copies, exposed the pamphlets in a basket at a penny apiece. The same little book has been recently sold by auction for twenty-one guineas!

Nine years elapsed before FitzGerald was moved to undertake another edition of his " Rubáiyát." In that time M. Nicolas, French Consul at Resht and Interpreter at the Court of Teheran, had under the auspices and with the aid of some learned and extravagant Sufi, brought out in Paris the text and a prose translation of 464 of the quatrains (Paris, 1867,) and FitzGerald, though interested in the Sufistic interpretations of the lines referring to wine and debauchery, found himself *unable to accept them. In the preface to the second edition, which was published in 1868 with the number of the quatrains increased from seventy-five to 110 and with many modifications and changes, he vigorously combats the theory of mysticism and sees in Omar a sound and sensible philosopher, an able scientist and a hail-fellow well met.*

The second edition, which also appeared with paper covers and anonymously, attracted some attention on both sides of the water. Professor Charles Eliot Norton published a review of it, containing prose translations from the French version of M. Nicolas. This edition is now becoming very scarce and brings not less than thirty or thirty-five dollars. Many lovers of Omar prefer the second redaction to any other, though probably there is no one who does not think the first quatrain of the first edition in its Homeric splendour is vastly superior to its later variants.

The third edition was published in 1872 in a small quarto in half roan and with 101 quatrains, —a number unchanged in any later edition. From this was printed the first American edition in

1878. In 1879 came the fourth edition, in an octavo form, half roan, with the "Salámán and Absál" cut down about one-half from its original size, thickening the book to 112 pages. It had as a frontispiece the engraved reproduction of a Persian picture of the royal game of Chugán or polo. In this edition the reference to Nicolas in the Preface is omitted and there are no note-numbers in the text. Both of these editions are becoming scarce. FitzGerald died on the fourteenth of June, 1883, and the following year Mr. Elihu Vedder brought out his splendid series of illustrations in an imperial quarto. This work probably did more than anything else to make the poem widely known. From that time forth it took its place as an English as well as a Persian classic. In 1887, four years after FitzGerald's death, Bernard Quaritch of London, in coöperation with Houghton, Mifflin & Company of New York and Boston, published a memorial edition of the works of Edward FitzGerald edited by Michael Kerney, who hid his identity under the name of Mimkaf, a compound of his initials in Persian. Mr. Kerney furnished a biograph-

*ical introduction and some tributary stanzas. The
first and fourth editions of the Rubáiyát are reprinted in the first volume on opposite pages com-
paratively arranged, and Mr. Kerney supple-
mented FitzGerald's notes with a series of his own
notes* "*giving references from Fitzgerald's Rubáiyát to the originals as published by Nicolas, Paris,
1867, and Mr. Whinfield's English version,
printed in 1882, with occasional literal renderings
in the form and metre of the originals.*" *The number of the quatrains rendered by Mr. Kerney is
exactly fifty. This edition might possibly be termed
the Fifth, but as it varies from the Fourth only
by correcting* her's *to* hers *in the fourth line of
the sixth stanza, in omitting three commas (xxiii,
line* 1, and we, that ; *xxv,* 2, stare, ; *lxv,* 4, comrades, and), *in printing in the fourth line of R.
xciii* reputation *for* Reputation ; *and in evidently
misprinting* such a cloud *for* such a clod *in the
third line of the thirty-eighth, it may be safely
considered as the same as the Fourth. The Fifth
then is that text which is included in the three-vol-
ume edition edited by Dr. W. Aldis Wright of*

Trinity College, Cambridge, to whom FitzGerald left a tin box containing various literary remains and among other things a copy of the Fourth Edition with a few verbal changes. He had also the first draught of the Third Edition, which varies slightly from that printed.

The present edition, which, so far as texts are concerned, may be regarded as definitive, contains the reprint of the First, Second and Fifth, carefully compared with the originals. The variants of the first draught of the Third are taken from Dr. Wright's edition. The editor has compared line for line and word for word the Third and Fourth Editions with the Kerney and Wright reprints and has noted one or two interesting variants hitherto not detected. No pains have been spared to make the work absolutely accurate, and thus the reader has all of FitzGerald's work on the Rubáiyát in convenient shape for reference and comparison. Students of Omar will of course still require the Multivariorum Edition in which about thirty versions in English, French, German and Italian are represented, and the literal translation by Edward

Heron-Allen of the Bodleian MS., which, together with a transliteration, is reproduced in one noble volume full of the richest Omarian lore. But Fitz-Gerald has thousands of votaries and the present edition, it is believed, attains the high-water mark of beauty and convenience.

NATHAN HASKELL DOLE.

OMAR KHAYYÁM
THE ASTRONOMER-
POET OF PERSIA

OMAR KHAYYÁM

THE

ASTRONOMER-POET OF PERSIA

BY EDWARD FITZGERALD

OMAR Khayyám was born at Naishápúr in Khorassán in the latter half of our Eleventh, and died within the First Quarter of our Twelfth Century. The slender Story of his Life is curiously twined about that of two other very considerable Figures in their Time and Country: one of whom tells the Story of all Three. This was Nizám ul Mulk, Vizyr to Alp Arslan the Son, and Malik Shah the Grandson, of Toghrul Beg the Tartar, who had wrested Persia from the feeble Successor of Mahmúd the Great, and founded that Seljukian Dynasty which finally roused Europe into the Crusades. This Nizám ul Mulk, in his *Wasiyat*—or *Testament*—which he wrote and left as a Memorial for future Statesmen —relates the following, as quoted in the *Calcutta Review*, No. 59, from Mirkhond's History of the Assassins.

"'One of the greatest of the wise men of Kho-
'rassán was the Imám Mowaffak of Naishápúr, a
'man highly honoured and reverenced,—may
'God rejoice his soul; his illustrious years exceeded
'eighty-five, and it was the universal belief that
'every boy who read the Koran or studied the tra-
'ditions in his presence, would assuredly attain to
'honour and happiness. For this cause did my fa-
'ther send me from Tús to Naishápúr with Abd-
'us-samad, the doctor of law, that I might employ
'myself in study and learning under the guidance
'of that illustrious teacher. Towards me he ever
'turned an eye of favour and kindness, and as his
'pupil I felt for him extreme affection and devo-
'tion, so that I passed four years in his service.
'When I first came there, I found two other pu-
'pils of mine own age newly arrived, Hakim Omar
'Khayyám, and the ill-fated Ben Sabbáh. Both
'were endowed with sharpness of wit and the
'highest natural powers; and we three formed a
'close friendship together. When the Imám rose
'from his lectures, they used to join me, and we
'repeated to each other the lessons we had heard.
'Now Omar was a native of Naishápúr, while

'Hasan Ben Sabbáh's father was one Ali, a man of
'austere life and practice, but heretical in his creed
'and doctrine. One day Hasan said to me and to
'Khayyám, 'It is a universal belief that the pupils
'of the Imám Mowaffak will attain to fortune.
'Now, even if we *all* do not attain thereto, with-
'out doubt one of us will ; what then shall be our
'mutual pledge and bond?' We answered, 'Be it
'what you please.' 'Well,' he said, 'let us make a
'vow, that to whomsoever this fortune falls, he
'shall share it equally with the rest, and reserve
'no pre-eminence for himself.' 'Be it so,' we both
'replied, and on those terms we mutually pledged
'our words. Years rolled on, and I went from Kho-
'rassán to Transoxiana, and wandered to Ghazni
'and Cabul ; and when I returned, I was invested
'with office, and rose to be administrator of af-
'fairs during the Sultanate of Sultan Alp Arslán.'
"He goes on to state, that years passed by, and
both his old school-friends found him out, and
came and claimed a share in his good fortune, according to the school-day vow. The Vizier was
generous and kept his word. Hasan demanded a
place in the government, which the Sultan granted

at the Vizier's request; but discontented with a gradual rise, he plunged into the maze of intrigue of an oriental court, and, failing in a base attempt to supplant his benefactor, he was disgraced and fell. After many mishaps and wanderings, Hasan became the head of the Persian sect of the *Ismailians*, — a party of fanatics who had long murmured in obscurity, but rose to an evil eminence under the guidance of his strong and evil will. In A.D. 1090, he seized the castle of Alamút, in the province of Rúdbar, which lies in the mountainous tract south of the Caspian Sea; and it was from this mountain home he obtained that evil celebrity among the Crusaders as the OLD MAN OF THE MOUNTAINS, and spread terror through the Mohammedan world; and it is yet disputed whether the word *Assassin*, which they have left in the language of modern Europe as their dark memorial, is derived from the *hashish*, or opiate of hemp-leaves (the Indian *bhang*), with which they maddened themselves to the sullen pitch of oriental desperation, or from the name of the founder of the dynasty, whom we have seen in his quiet collegiate days, at Naishápúr. One of the countless victims of the Assassin's dagger was Nizám-ul-Mulk himself, the old school-boy friend.*

"Omar Khayyám also came to the Vizier to claim his share; but not to ask for title or office. 'The 'greatest boon you can confer on me,' he said, 'is 'to let me live in a corner under the shadow of 'your fortune, to spread wide the advantages of 'Science, and pray for your long life and prosper-'ity.' The Vizier tells us, that, when he found Omar was really sincere in his refusal, he pressed him no further, but granted him a yearly pension of 1200 *mithkáls* of gold, from the treasury of Naishápúr.

"At Naishápúr thus lived and died Omar Khay-yám, 'busied,' adds the Vizier, 'in winning know-'ledge of every kind, and especially in Astronomy, 'wherein he attained to a very high pre-eminence. 'Under the Sultanate of Malik Shah, he came to

---

* Some of Omar's Rubáiyát warn us of the danger of Greatness, the instability of Fortune, and while advocating Charity to all Men, recommending us to be too intimate with none. Attár makes Nizám-ul-Mulk use the very words of his friend Omar [Rub. xxviii], "When Nizám-ul-Mulk was in the Agony (of Death) he said, 'Oh God! I am passing away in the hand of the wind.'"

[27]

'Merv, and obtained great praise for his profi-
'ciency in science, and the Sultan showered fa-
'vours upon him.'

"When Malik Shah determined to reform the calendar, Omar was one of the eight learned men employed to do it; the result was the *Jaláli* era (so
called from *Jalál-ud-din*, one of the king's names)
—'a computation of time,' says Gibbon, 'which
'surpasses the Julian, and approaches the accuracy of
'the Gregorian style.' He is also the author of some
astronomical tables, entitled Zíji-Maliksháhí," and
the French have lately republished and translated
an Arabic Treatise of his on Algebra.

"His Takhallus or poetical name (Khayyám) signifies a Tent-maker, and he is said to have at one
time exercised that trade, perhaps before Nizám-
ul-Mulk's generosity raised him to independence.
Many Persian poets similarly derive their names
from their occupations; thus we have Attár, 'a
druggist,' Assár, 'an oil presser,' etc.* Omar him-

---

* Though all these, like our Smiths, Archers, Millers,
Fletchers, etc., may simply retain the Surname of an
hereditary calling.

self alludes to his name in the following whimsical lines :—

'Khayyám, who stitched the tents of science,
Has fallen in grief's furnace and been suddenly burned;
The shears of Fate have cut the tent ropes of his life,
And the broker of Hope has sold him for nothing!'

"We have only one more anecdote to give of his Life, and that relates to the close; it is told in the anonymous preface which is sometimes prefixed to his poems; it has been printed in the Persian in the Appendix to Hyde's *Veterum Persarum Religio*, p. 499; and D'Herbelot alludes to it in his Bibliothèque, under *Khiam.*—*

"'It is written in the chronicles of the ancients 'that this King of the Wise, Omar Khayyám, died 'at Naishápúr in the year of the Hegira, 517 (A.D. '1123); in science he was unrivalled,—the very 'paragon of his age. Khwájah Nizámi of Samar-'cand, who was one of his pupils, relates the fol-

---

* "*Philosophe Musulman qui a vécu en Odeur de Sainteté dans sa Religion, vers la Fin du premir et la Commencement du Siècle,*" no part of which, except the *Philosophe,* can apply to our Khayyám.

[29]

'lowing story: 'I often used to hold conversations 'with my teacher, Omar Khayyám, in a garden; 'and one day he said to me, 'My tomb shall be in 'a spot where the north wind may scatter roses 'over it.' I wondered at the words he spake, but I 'knew that his were no idle words.* Years after,

---

* The Rashness of the Words, according to D'Herbelot, consisted in being so opposed to those in the Korán: "No Man knows where he shall die."—This story of Omar reminds me of another so naturally—and when one remembers how wide of his humble mark the noble sailor aimed—so pathetically told by Captain Cook— not by Doctor Hawkesworth—in his Second Voyage (i. 374). When leaving Ulietea, " Oreo's last request was for me to return. When he saw he could not obtain that promise, he asked the name of my *Marai* (burying-place). As strange a question as this was, I hesitated not a moment to tell him 'Stepney;' the parish in which I live when in London. I was made to repeat it several times over till they could pronounce it; and then 'Stepney Marai no Toote' was echoed through an hundred mouths at once. I afterwards found the same question had been put to Mr. Forster by a man on shore; but he gave a different, and indeed more proper answer, by saying, 'No man who used the sea could say where he should be buried.'"

[30]

'when I chanced to revisit Naishápúr, I went to
'his final resting-place, and lo! it was just outside
'a garden, and trees laden with fruit stretched
'their boughs over the garden wall, and dropped
'their flowers upon his tomb, so that the stone was
'hidden under them.'"

Thus far—without fear of Trespass—from the
Calcutta Review. The writer of it, on reading in
India this story of Omar's Grave, was reminded, he
says, of Cicero's Account of finding Archimedes'
Tomb at Syracuse, buried in grass and weeds. I
think Thorwaldsen desired to have roses grow over
him; a wish religiously fulfilled for him to the present day, I believe. However, to return to Omar.
Though the Sultan "shower'd Favours upon him,"
Omar's Epicurean Audacity of Thought and Speech
caused him to be regarded askance in his own Time
and Country. He is said to have been especially
hated and dreaded by the Súfis, whose Practice he
ridiculed, and whose Faith amounted to little more
than his own, when stript of the Mysticism and
formal recognition of Islamism under which Omar
would not hide. Their Poets, including Háfiz, who
are (with the exception of Firdausi) the most con-

siderable in Persia, borrowed largely, indeed, of
Omar's material, but turning it to a mystical Use
more convenient to Themselves and the People
they addressed; a People quite as quick of Doubt
as of Belief; as keen of Bodily Sense as of Intel-
lectual; and delighting in a cloudy composition of
both, in which they could float luxuriously between
Heaven and Earth, and this World and the Next,
on the wings of a poetical expression, that might
serve indifferently for either. Omar was too honest
of Heart as well as of Head for this. Having failed
(however mistakenly) of finding any Providence
but Destiny, and any World but This, he set about
making the most of it; preferring rather to soothe
the Soul through the Senses into Acquiescence
with Things as he saw them, than to perplex it
with vain disquietude after what they *might* be. It
has been seen, however, that his Worldly Ambition was not exorbitant; and he very likely takes
a humorous or perverse pleasure in exalting the
gratification of Sense above that of the Intellect, in
which he must have taken great delight, although
it failed to answer the Questions in which he, in
common with all men, was most vitally interested.

[32]

For whatever Reason, however, Omar, as before said, has never been popular in his own Country, and therefore has been but scantily transmitted abroad. The MSS. of his Poems, mutilated beyond the average Casualties of Oriental Transcription, are so rare in the East as scarce to have reacht Westward at all, in spite of all the acquisitions of Arms and Science. There is no copy at the India House, none at the Bibliothèque Nationale of Paris. We know but of one in England : No. 140 of the Ouseley MSS. at the Bodleian, written at Shiráz, A.D. 1460. This contains but 158 Rubáiyát. One in the Asiatic Society's Library at Calcutta (of which we have a Copy), contains (and yet incomplete) 516, though swelled to that by all kinds of Repetition and Corruption. So Von Hammer speaks of *his* Copy as containing about 200, while Dr. Sprenger catalogues the Lucknow MS. at double that number.* The Scribes, too, of the Oxford and Calcutta

* "Since this paper was written" (adds the Reviewer in a note), "we have met with a Copy of a very rare Edition, printed at Calcutta in 1836. This contains 438 Tetrastichs, with an Appendix containing 54 others not found in some MSS."

MSS. seem to do their Work under a sort of Protest; each beginning with a Tetrastich (whether genuine or not), taken out of its alphabetical order; the Oxford with one of Apology; the Calcutta with one of Expostulation, supposed (says a Notice prefixed to the MS.) to have arisen from a Dream, in which Omar's mother asked about his future fate. It may be rendered thus:—

> *" Oh Thou who burn'st in Heart for those who burn*
> *" In Hell, whose fires thyself shall feed in turn;*
> *" How long be crying, ' Mercy on them, God!'*
> *" Why, who art Thou to teach, and He to learn? "*

The Bodleian Quatrain pleads Pantheism by way of Justification.

> *" If I myself upon a looser Creed*
> *" Have loosely strung the Jewel of Good deed,*
> *" Let this one thing for my Atonement plead:*
> *" That One for Two I never did mis-read."*

The Reviewer,* to whom I owe the Particulars of Omar's Life, concludes his Review by comparing him with Lucretius, both as to natural Temper and Genius, and as acted upon by the Circum-

---

* Professor Cowell.

stances in which he lived. Both indeed were men of subtle, strong, and cultivated Intellect, fine Imagination, and Hearts passionate for Truth and Justice; who justly revolted from their Country's false Religion, and false, or foolish, Devotion to it; but who fell short of replacing what they subverted by such better *Hope* as others, with no better Revelation to guide them, had yet made a Law to themselves. Lucretius, indeed, with such material as Epicurus furnished, satisfied himself with the theory of a vast machine fortuitously constructed, and acting by a Law that implied no Legislator; and so composing himself into a Stoical rather than Epicurean severity of Attitude, sat down to contemplate the mechanical Drama of the Universe which he was part Actor in; himself and all about him (as in his own sublime description of the Roman Theatre) discoloured with the lurid reflex of the Curtain suspended between the Spectator and the Sun. Omar, more desperate, or more careless of any so complicated System as resulted in nothing but hopeless Necessity, flung his own Genius and Learning with a bitter or humorous jest into the general Ruin which their insufficient glimpses only served to reveal ; and, pretending sensual pleasure as the serious purpose of Life, only *diverted* himself with speculative problems of Deity, Destiny, Matter and Spirit, Good and Evil, and other such questions, easier to start than to run down, and the pursuit of which becomes a very weary sport at last !

With regard to the present Translation. The original Rubáiyát (as, missing an Arabic Guttural, these *Tetrastichs* are more musically called) are independent Stanzas, consisting each of four Lines of equal, though varied, Prosody ; sometimes *all* rhyming, but oftener (as here imitated) the third line a blank. Somewhat as in the Greek Alcaic, where the penultimate line seems to lift and suspend the Wave that falls over in the last. As usual with such kind of Oriental Verse, the Rubáiyát follow one another according to Alphabetic Rhyme— a strange succession of Grave and Gay. Those here selected are strung into something of an Eclogue, with perhaps a less than equal proportion of the "Drink and make-merry," which (genuine or not) recurs over-frequently in the Original.

Either way, the Result is sad enough : saddest perhaps when most ostentatiously merry : more apt to move Sorrow than Anger toward the old Tentmaker, who, after vainly endeavouring to un-shackle his Steps from Destiny, and to catch some authentic Glimpse of To-morrow, fell back upon To-day (which has outlasted so many To-mor-rows!) as the only Ground he had got to stand upon, however momentarily slipping from under his Feet.

(FROM THE THIRD EDITION)

WHILE the second Edition of this version of Omar was preparing, Monsieur Nicolas, French Consul at Resht, published a very careful and very good Edition of the Text, from a litho-graph copy at Teheran, comprising 464 Rubáiyát, with translation and notes of his own.
Mons. Nicolas, whose Edition has reminded me of several things, and instructed me in others, does not consider Omar to be the material Epicurean that I have literally taken him for, but a Mystic, shadowing the Deity under the figure of Wine,

Wine-bearer, &c., as Háfiz is supposed to do; in short, a Súfi Poet like Háfiz and the rest.

I cannot see reason to alter my opinion, formed as it was more than a dozen years ago* when Omar was first shown me by one to whom I am indebted for all I know of Oriental, and very much of other, literature. He admired Omar's Genius so much, that he would gladly have adopted any such Interpretation of his meaning as Mons. Nicolas' if he could.† That he could not, appears by his Paper in the Calcutta Review already so largely quoted; in which he argues from the Poems themselves, as well as from what records remain of the Poet's Life. And if more were needed to disprove Mons. Nicolas' Theory, there is the Biographical Notice which he himself has drawn up in direct contradiction to the Interpretation of the Poems given in his Notes. (See pp. xiii–xiv of his Preface.) Indeed I hardly knew poor Omar was so far gone till his Apologist informed me. For here we see that whatever were

---

* [This was written in 1868. W. A. W.]

† Perhaps would have edited the Poems himself some years ago. He may now as little approve of my Version on one side, as of Mons. Nicolas' Theory on the other.

[38]

the Wine that Háfiz drank and sang, the verita-
ble Juice of the Grape it was which Omar used,
not only when carousing with his friends, but (says
Mons. Nicolas) in order to excite himself to that
pitch of Devotion which others reached by cries
and "hurlemens." And yet, whenever Wine,
Wine-bearer, &c., occur in the text — which is
often enough — Mons. Nicolas carefully annotates
"Dieu," "La Divinité," &c. : so carefully indeed
that one is tempted to think that he was indoctri-
nated by the Súfi with whom he read the Poems.
(Note to Rub. ii. p. 8.) A Persian would naturally
wish to vindicate a distinguished Countryman ;
and a Súfi to enrol him in his own sect, which
already comprises all the chief Poets of Persia.
What historical Authority has Mons. Nicolas to
show that Omar gave himself up "avec passion à
l'étude de la philosophie des Soufis ?" (Preface,
p. xiii.) The Doctrines of Pantheism, Material-
ism, Necessity, &c., were not peculiar to the Súfi ;
nor to Lucretius before them ; nor to Epicurus
before him ; probably the very original Irreligion
of Thinking men from the first ; and very likely
to be the spontaneous growth of a Philosopher

living in an Age of social and political barbarism,
under shadow of one of the Two and Seventy Religions supposed to divide the world. Von Hammer
(according to Sprenger's Oriental Catalogue) speaks
of Omar as "a Free-thinker, and *a great opponent of
Sufism;*" perhaps because, while holding much
of their Doctrine, he would not pretend to any
inconsistent severity of morals. Sir W. Ouseley has
written a note to something of the same effect on
the fly-leaf of the Bodleian MS. And in two Rubáiyát of Mons. Nicolas' own Edition Súf and
Súfi are both disparagingly named.

No doubt many of these Quatrains seem unaccountable unless mystically interpreted ; but many
more as unaccountable unless literally. Were the
Wine spiritual, for instance, how wash the Body
with it when dead? Why make cups of the dead
clay to be filled with — "La Divinité" — by some
succeeding Mystic? Mons. Nicolas himself is puz-
zled by some "bizarres" and "trop Orientales"
allusions and images — "d'une sensualité quelquefois révoltante" indeed — which "les conve-
nances" do not permit him to translate ; but still
which the reader cannot but refer to "La Divi-

nité."* No doubt also many of the Quatrains in the Teheran, as in the Calcutta, Copies, are spurious; such *Rubáiyát* being the common form of Epigram in Persia. But this, at best, tells as much one way as another; nay, the Súfi, who may be considered the Scholar and Man of Letters in Persia, would be far more likely than the careless Epicure to interpolate what favours his own view of the Poet. I observe that very few of the more mystical Quatrains are in the Bodleian MS. which must

---

* A Note to Quatrain 234 admits that, however clear the mystical meaning of such Images must be to Europeans, they are not quoted without "rougissant" even by laymen in Persia—"*Quant aux termes de tendresse qui commencent ce quatrain, comme tant d'autres dans ce recueil, nos lecteurs, habitués maintenant à l'étrangeté des expressions si souvent employés par Khéyam pour rendre ses pensées sur l'amour divin, et à la singularité de ses images trop orientales, d'une sensualité quelquefois révoltante, n'auront pas de peine à se persuader qu'il s'agit de la Divinité, bien que cette conviction soit vivement discutée par les moullahs musulmans et même par beaucoup de laïques, qui rougissent véritablement d'une pareille licence de leur compatriote à l'égard des choses spirituelles.*"

be one of the oldest, as dated at Shiraz, A. H. 865, A. D. 1460. And this, I think, especially distinguishes Omar (I cannot help calling him by his — no, not Christian — familiar name) from all other Persian Poets : That, whereas with them the Poet is lost in his Song, the Man in Allegory and Abstraction ; we seem to have the Man — the *Bon-homme* — Omar himself, with all his Humours and Passions, as frankly before us as if we were really at Table with him, after the Wine had gone round. I must say that I, for one, never wholly believed in the Mysticism of Háfiz. It does not appear there was any danger in holding and singing Súfi Pantheism, so long as the Poet made his Salaam to Mohammed at the beginning and end of his Song. Under such conditions Jeláluddín, Jámí, Attár, and others sang ; using Wine and Beauty indeed as Images to illustrate, not as a Mask to hide, the Divinity they were celebrating. Perhaps some Allegory less liable to mistake or abuse had been better among so inflammable a People : much more so when, as some think with Háfiz and Omar, the abstract is not only likened to, but identified with, the sensual Image ; hazardous, if not to the Devotee himself, yet to his weaker Brethren; and worse for the Profane in proportion as the Devotion of the Initiated grew warmer. And all for what? To be tantalized with Images of sensual enjoyment which must be renounced if one would approximate a God, who according to the Doctrine, *is* Sensual Matter as well as Spirit, and into whose Universe one expects unconsciously to merge after Death, without hope of any posthumous Beatitude in another world to compensate for all one's self-denial in this. Lucretius' blind Divinity certainly merited, and probably got, as much self-sacrifice as this of the Súfi; and the burden of Omar's Song —if not "Let us eat"—is assuredly—"Let us drink, for To-morrow we die!" And if Háfiz meant quite otherwise by a similar language, he surely miscalculated when he devoted his Life and Genius to so equivocal a Psalmody as, from his Day to this, has been said and sung by any rather than Spiritual Worshippers.

However, as there is some traditional presumption, and certainly the opinion of some learned men, in favour of Omar's being a Súfi—and even something of a Saint—those who please may so inter-

pret his Wine and Cup-bearer. On the other hand,
as there is far more historical certainty of his being
a Philosopher, of scientific Insight and Ability far
beyond that of the Age and Country he lived in;
of such moderate worldly Ambition as becomes a
Philosopher, and such moderate wants as rarely
satisfy a Debauchee; other readers may be content
to believe with me that, while the Wine Omar
celebrates is simply the Juice of the Grape, he
bragged more than he drank of it, in very defiance
perhaps of that Spiritual Wine which left its Votaries sunk in Hypocrisy or Disgust.

RUBÁIYÁT OF
OMAR KHAYYÁM

FIRST EDITION 1859

RUBÁIYÁT OF OMAR KHAYYÁM

FIRST EDITION
MDCCCLIX

I

AWAKE! for Morning in the Bowl of Night
　　Has flung the Stone that puts the Stars
　　　　to Flight:
And Lo! the Hunter of the East has caught
The Sultán's Turret in a Noose of Light.

II

Dreaming when Dawn's Left Hand was in the Sky
I heard a Voice within the Tavern cry,
　　"Awake, my Little ones, and fill the Cup
"Before Life's Liquor in its Cup be dry."

III

And, as the Cock crew, those who stood before
The Tavern shouted — "Open then the Door!
　　"You know how little while we have to stay,
"And, once departed, may return no more."

[47]

IV

Now the New Year reviving old Desires,
The thoughtful Soul to Solitude retires,
  Where the WHITE HAND OF MOSES on the Bough
Puts out, and Jesus from the Ground suspires.

V

Irám indeed is gone with all its Rose,
And Jamshýd's Sev'n-ring'd Cup where no one
    knows;
  But still the Vine her ancient Ruby yields,
And still a Garden by the Water blows.

VI

And David's Lips are lock't; but in divine
High piping Péhlevi, with "Wine! Wine! Wine!
  "*Red* Wine!"—the Nightingale cries to the
    Rose
That yellow Cheek of her's to 'incarnadine.

VII

Come, fill the Cup, and in the Fire of Spring
The Winter Garment of Repentance fling:
  The Bird of Time has but a little way
To fly—and Lo! the Bird is on the Wing.

[48]

VIII

And look—a thousand Blossoms with the Day
Woke—and a thousand scatter'd into Clay:
    And this first Summer Month that brings the
      Rose
Shall take Jamshýd and Kaikobád away.

IX

But come with old Khayyám, and leave the Lot
Of Kaikobád and Kaikhosrú forgot!
    Let Rustum lay about him as he will,
Or Hátim Tai cry Supper—heed them not.

X

With me along some Strip of Herbage strown
That just divides the desert from the sown,
    Where name of Slave and Sultán scarce is known,
And pity Sultán Máhmúd on his Throne.

XI

Here with a Loaf of Bread beneath the Bough,
A Flask of Wine, a Book of Verse—and Thou
    Beside me singing in the Wilderness—
And Wilderness is Paradise enow.

XII

"How sweet is mortal Sovranty!"—think some:
Others—"How blest the Paradise to come!"
   Ah, take the Cash in hand and waive the Rest;
Oh, the brave Music of a *distant* Drum!

XIII

Look to the Rose that blows about us—"Lo,
"Laughing," she says, "into the World I blow:
   "At once the silken Tassel of my Purse
"Tear, and its Treasure on the Garden throw."

XIV

The Worldly Hope men set their Hearts upon
Turns Ashes—or it prospers; and anon,
   Like Snow upon the Desert's dusty Face
Lighting a little Hour or two—is gone.

XV

And those who husbanded the Golden Grain,
And those who flung it to the Winds like Rain,
   Alike to no such aureate Earth are turn'd
As, buried once, Men want dug up again.

XVI

Think, in this batter'd Caravanserai
Whose Doorways are alternate Night and Day,
   How Sultán after Sultán with his Pomp
Abode his Hour or two, and went his way.

XVII

They say the Lion and the Lizard keep
The Courts where Jamshýd gloried and drank deep;
   And Bahrám, that great Hunter — the Wild Ass
Stamps o'er his Head, and he lies fast asleep.

XVIII

I sometimes think that never blows so red
The Rose as where some buried Cæsar bled;
   That every Hyacinth the Garden wears
Dropt in its Lap from some once lovely Head.

XIX

And this delightful Herb whose tender Green
Fledges the River's Lip on which we lean —
   Ah, lean upon it lightly! for who knows
From what once lovely Lip it springs unseen!

X X

Ah, my Belovéd, fill the Cup that clears
To-DAY of past Regrets and future Fears—
    To-morrow?—Why, To-morrow I may be
Myself with Yesterday's Sev'n Thousand Years.

X X I

Lo! some we loved, the loveliest and best
That Time and Fate of all their Vintage prest,
    Have drunk their Cup a Round or two before,
And one by one crept silently to Rest.

X X I I

And we, that now make merry in the Room
They left, and Summer dresses in new Bloom,
    Ourselves must we beneath the Couch of Earth
Descend, ourselves to make a Couch—for whom?

X X I I I

Ah, make the most of what we yet may spend,
Before we too into the Dust descend;
    Dust into Dust, and under Dust, to lie,
Sans Wine, sans Song, sans Singer, and—sans End!

XXIV

Alike for those who for To-day prepare,
And those that after a To-morrow stare,
   A Muezzín from the Tower of Darkness cries
"Fools! your Reward is neither Here nor There!"

XXV

Why, all the Saints and Sages who discuss'd
Of the Two Worlds so learnedly, are thrust
   Like foolish Prophets forth; their Words to Scorn
Are scatter'd, and their Mouths are stopt with Dust.

XXVI

Oh, come with old Khayyám, and leave the Wise
To talk; one thing is certain, that Life flies;
   One thing is certain, and the Rest is Lies;
The Flower that once has blown for ever dies.

XXVII

Myself when young did eagerly frequent
Doctor and Saint, and heard great Argument
   About it and about: but evermore
Came out by the same Door as in I went.

XXVIII

With them the Seed of Wisdom did I sow,
And with my own hand labour'd it to grow :
    And this was all the Harvest that I reap'd—
"I came like Water, and like Wind I go."

XXIX

Into this Universe, and *why* not knowing,
Nor *whence*, like Water willy-nilly flowing :
    And out of it, as Wind along the Waste,
I know not *whither*, willy-nilly blowing.

XXX

What, without asking, hither hurried *whence?*
And, without asking, *whither* hurried hence !
    Another and another Cup to drown
The Memory of this Impertinence !

XXXI

Up from Earth's Centre through the Seventh Gate
I rose, and on the Throne of Saturn sate,
    And many Knots unravel'd by the Road ;
But not the Knot of Human Death and Fate.

XXXII

There was a Door to which I found no Key:
There was a Veil past which I could not see:
   Some little Talk awhile of ME and THEE
There seemed—and then no more of THEE and
    ME.

XXXIII

Then to the rolling Heav'n itself I cried,
Asking, "What Lamp had Destiny to guide
   "Her little Children stumbling in the Dark?"
And—"A blind Understanding!" Heav'n replied.

XXXIV

Then to this earthen Bowl did I adjourn
My Lip the secret Well of Life to learn:
   And Lip to Lip it murmur'd—"While you live
"Drink!—for once dead you never shall return."

XXXV

I think the Vessel, that with fugitive
Articulation answer'd, once did live,
   And merry-make; and the cold Lip I kiss'd
How many Kisses might it take—and give!

XXXVI

For in the Market-place, one Dusk of Day,
I watch'd the Potter thumping his wet Clay:
    And with its all obliterated Tongue
It murmur'd — "Gently, Brother, gently, pray!"

XXXVII

Ah, fill the Cup: — what boots it to repeat
How Time is slipping underneath our Feet:
    Unborn TO-MORROW, and dead YESTERDAY,
Why fret about them if TO-DAY be sweet!

XXXVIII

One Moment in Annihilation's Waste,
One Moment, of the Well of Life to taste —
    The Stars are setting and the Caravan
Starts for the Dawn of Nothing — Oh, make haste!

XXXIX

How long, how long, in infinite Pursuit
Of This and That endeavour and dispute?
    Better be merry with the fruitful Grape
Than sadden after none, or bitter, Fruit.

X L

You know, my Friends, how long since in my
    House
For a new Marriage I did make Carouse:
    Divorced old barren Reason from my Bed,
And took the Daughter of the Vine to Spouse.

X L I

For "Is" and "Is-not" though *with* Rule and Line,
And "Up-and-down" *without*, I could define,
    I yet in all I only cared to know,
Was never deep in anything but—Wine.

X L I I

And lately, by the Tavern Door agape,
Came stealing through the Dusk an Angel Shape
    Bearing a Vessel on his Shoulder; and
He bid me taste of it; and 'twas—the Grape!

X L I I I

The Grape that can with Logic absolute
The Two-and-Seventy jarring Sects confute:
    The subtle Alchemist that in a Trice
Life's leaden Metal into Gold transmute.

XLIV

The mighty Mahmúd, the victorious Lord,
That all the misbelieving and black Horde
  Of Fears and Sorrows that infest the Soul
Scatters and slays with his enchanted Sword.

XLV

But leave the Wise to wrangle, and with me
The Quarrel of the Universe let be:
  And, in some corner of the Hubbub coucht,
Make Game of that which makes as much of Thee.

XLVI

For in and out, above, about, below,
'Tis nothing but a Magic Shadow-show,
  Play'd in a Box whose Candle is the Sun,
Round which we Phantom Figures come and go.

XLVII

And if the Wine you drink, the Lip you press,
End in the Nothing all Things end in — Yes —
  Then fancy while Thou art, Thou art but what
Thou shalt be — Nothing — Thou shalt not be less.

XLVIII

While the Rose blows along the River Brink,
With old Khayyám the Ruby Vintage drink:
    And when the Angel with his darker Draught
Draws up to Thee—take that, and do not shrink.

XLIX

'Tis all a Chequer-board of Nights and Days
Where Destiny with Men for Pieces plays:
    Hither and thither moves, and mates, and slays,
And one by one back in the Closet lays.

L

The Ball no Question makes of Ayes and Noes,
But Right or Left, as strikes the Player goes;
    And He that toss'd Thee down into the Field,
He knows about it all—HE knows—HE knows!

LI

The Moving Finger writes; and, having writ,
Moves on: nor all thy Piety nor Wit
    Shall lure it back to cancel half a Line,
Nor all thy Tears wash out a Word of it.

LII

And that inverted Bowl we call The Sky,
Whereunder crawling coop't we live and die,
    Lift not thy hands to *It* for help — for It
Rolls impotently on as Thou or I.

LIII

With Earth's first Clay They did the Last Man's
        knead,
And then of the Last Harvest sow'd the Seed:
    Yea, the first Morning of Creation wrote
What the Last Dawn of Reckoning shall read.

LIV

I tell Thee this — When, starting from the Goal,
Over the shoulders of the flaming Foal
    Of Heav'n Parwín and Mushtara they flung,
In my predestin'd Plot of Dust and Soul

LV

The Vine had struck a Fibre; which about
If clings my Being — let the Súfi flout;
    Of my Base Metal may be filed a Key,
That shall unlock the Door he howls without.

LVI

And this I know: whether the one True Light,
Kindle to Love, or Wrathconsume me quite,
   One Glimpse of It within the Tavern caught
Better than in the Temple lost outright.

LVII

Oh, Thou, who didst with Pitfall and with Gin
Beset the Road I was to wander in,
   Thou wilt not with Predestination round
Enmesh me, and impute my Fall to Sin?

LVIII

Oh, Thou, who Man of baser Earth didst make,
And who with Eden didst devise the Snake;
   For all the Sin wherewith the Face of Man
Is blacken'd, Man's Forgiveness give—and take!

*   *   *   *   *   *   *

KÚZA-NÁMA*

LIX

Listen again. One Evening at the Close
Of Ramazán, ere the better Moon arose,
In that old Potter's Shop I stood alone
With the clay Population round in Rows.

LX

And, strange to tell, among that Earthen Lot
Some could articulate, while others not:
And suddenly one more impatient cried—
"Who *is* the Potter, pray, and who the Pot?"

LXI

Then said another—"Surely not in vain
"My Substance from the common Earth was ta'en,
"That He who subtly wrought me into Shape
"Should stamp me back to common Earth again."

---

* "*Book of Pots.*"

LXII

Another said—"Why, ne'er a peevish Boy,
"Would break the Bowl from which he drank in
    Joy;
  "Shall He that *made* the Vessel in pure Love
"And Fansy, in an after Rage destroy!"

LXIII

None answer'd this; but after Silence spake
A Vessel of a more ungainly Make:
  "They sneer at me for leaning all awry;
"What! did the Hand then of the Potter shake?"

LXIV

Said one—"Folks of a surly Tapster tell,
"And daub his Visage with the Smoke of Hell;
  "They talk of some strict Testing of us—Pish!
"He's a Good Fellow, and 't will all be well."

LXV

Then said another with a long-drawn Sigh,
"My Clay with long oblivion is gone dry:
  "But, fill me with the old familiar Juice,
"Methinks I might recover by-and-bye!"

[63]

LXVI

So while the Vessels one by one were speaking,
One spied the little Crescent all were seeking:
   And then they jogg'd each other, "Brother!
    Brother!
"Hark to the Porter's Shoulder-knot a-creaking!"

*   *   *   *   *   *   *

LXVII

Ah, with the Grape my fading Life provide,
And wash my Body whence the Life has died,
   And in the Windingsheet of Vine-leaf
    wrapt,
So bury me by some sweet Garden-side.

LXVIII

That ev'n my buried Ashes such a Snare
Of Perfume shall fling up into the Air,
   As not a True Believer passing by
But shall be overtaken unaware.

LXIX

Indeed the Idols I have loved so long
Have done my Credit in Men's Eye much wrong:
　　Have drown'd my Honour in a shallow Cup,
And sold my Reputation for a Song.

LXX

Indeed, indeed, Repentance oft before
I swore—but was I sober when I swore?
　　And then and then came Spring, and Rose-in-
　　　　hand
My thread-bare Penitence apieces tore.

LXXI

And much as Wine has play'd the Infidel,
And robb'd me of my Robe of Honour—well,
　　I often wonder what the Vintners buy
One half so precious as the Goods they sell.

LXXII

Alas, that Spring should vanish with the Rose!
That Youth's sweet-scented Manuscript should
　　　　close!
　　The Nightingale that in the Branches sang,
Ah, whence, and whither flown again, who knows!

LXXIII

Ah Love! could thou and I with Fate conspire
To grasp this sorry Scheme of Things entire,
   Would not we shatter it to bits—and then
Re-mould it nearer to the Heart's Desire!

LXXIV

Ah, Moon of my Delight who know'st no wane,
The Moon of Heav'n is rising once again:
   How oft hereafter rising shall she look
Through this same Garden after me—in vain!

LXXV

And when Thyself with shining Foot shall pass
Among the Guests Star-scatter'd on the Grass,
   And in thy joyous Errand reach the Spot
Where I made one—turn down an empty Glass!

_TAMÁM SHUD_*

---

* _It is completed._

RUBÁIYÁT OF
OMAR KHAYYÁM
OF NAISHÁPÚR

SECOND EDITION 1868

RUBÁIYÁT of OMAR KHAYYÁM OF NAISHÁPÚR

SECOND EDITION
MDCCCLXVIII

I

WAKE! For the Sun behind yon Eastern
height   [from Night,
Has chased the Session of the Stars
And, to the field of Heav'n ascending, strikes
The Sultán's Turret with a Shaft of Light.

II

Before the phantom of False morning died,
Methought a Voice within the Tavern cried,
  "When all the Temple is prepared within,
"Why lags the drowsy Worshipper outside?"

III

And, as the Cock crew, those who stood before
The Tavern shouted—"Open then the Door!
  "You know how little while we have to stay,
"And, once departed, may return **no more.**"

[69]

IV

Now the New Year reviving old Desires,
The thoughtful Soul to Solitude retires,
  Where the WHITE HAND OF MOSES on the Bough
Puts out, and Jesus from the ground suspires.

V

Iram indeed is gone with all his Rose,
And Jamshýd's Sev'n-ring'd Cup where no one
    knows;
  But still a Ruby gushes from the Vine,
And many a Garden by the Water blows.

VI

And David's lips are lockt; but in divine
High-piping Péhlevi, with "Wine! Wine! Wine!
  "Red Wine!"—the Nightingale cries to the
    Rose
That sallow cheek of her's to incarnadine.

VII

Come, fill the Cup, and in the fire of Spring
Your Winter-garment of Repentance fling:
  The Bird of Time has but a little way
To flutter—and the Bird is on the Wing.

VIII

Whether at Naishápúr or Babylon,
Whether the Cup with sweet or bitter run,
   The Wine of Life keeps oozing drop by drop,
The Leaves of Life keep falling one by one.

IX

Morning a thousand Roses brings, you say;
Yes, but where leaves the Rose of yesterday?
   And this first Summer month that brings the
     Rose
Shall take Jamshýd and Kaikobád away.

X

Well, let it take them! What have we to do
With Kaikobád the Great, or Kaikhosrú?
   Let Rustum cry "To Battle" as he likes,
Or Hátim Tai "To Supper!"—heed not you.

XI

With me along the strip of Herbage strown
That just divides the desert from the sown,
   Where name of Slave and Sultán is forgot—
And Peace to Máhmúd on his golden Throne!

XII

Here with a little Bread beneath the Bough,
A Flask of Wine, a Book of Verse—and Thou
    Beside me singing in the Wilderness—
Oh, Wilderness were Paradise enow!

XIII

Some for the Glories of This World; and some
Sigh for the Prophet's Paradise to come;
    Ah, take the Cash, and let the Promise go,
Nor heed the rumble of a distant Drum!

XIV

Were it not Folly, Spider-like to spin
The Thread of present Life away to win
    What? for ourselves, who know not if we shall
Breathe out the very Breath we now breathe in!

XV

Look to the blowing Rose about us—"Lo,
"Laughing," she says, "into the world I blow:
    "At once the silken tassel of my Purse
"Tear, and its Treasure on the Garden throw."

XVI

For those who husbanded the Golden grain,
And those who flung it to the winds like Rain,
   Alike to no such aureate Earth are turn'd
As, buried once, Men want dug up again.

XVII

The Worldly Hope men set their Hearts upon
Turns Ashes—or it prospers; and anon,
   Like Snow upon the Desert's dusty Face,
Lighting a little hour or two—was gone.

XVIII

Think, in this batter'd Caravanserai
Whose Portals are alternate Night and Day,
   How Sultán after Sultán with his Pomp
Abode his destin'd Hour, and went his way.

XIX

They say the Lion and the Lizard keep
The Courts where Jamshýd gloried and drank
    deep:
   And Bahrám, that great Hunter—the Wild Ass
Stamps o'er his Head, but cannot break his Sleep.

XX

The Palace that to Heav'n his pillars threw,
And Kings the forehead on his threshold drew—
   I saw the solitary Ringdove there,
And "Coo, coo, coo," she cried; and "Coo, coo,
     coo."

XXI

Ah, my Belovéd, fill the Cup that clears
To-DAY of past Regrets and future Fears:
   To-morrow!—Why, To-morrow I may be
Myself with Yesterday's Sev'n thousand Years.

XXII

For some we loved, the loveliest and the best
That from his Vintage rolling Time has prest,
   Have drunk their Cup a Round or two before,
And one by one crept silently to rest.

XXIII

And we, that now make merry in the Room
They left, and Summer dresses in new Bloom,
   Ourselves must we beneath the Couch of Earth
Descend, ourselves to make a Couch—for whom?

XXIV

I sometimes think that never blows so red
The Rose as where some buried Cæsar bled;
   That every Hyacinth the Garden wears
Dropt in her Lap from some once lovely Head.

XXV

And this delightful Herb whose living Green
Fledges the River's Lip on which we lean —
   Ah, lean upon it lightly! for who knows
From what once lovely Lip it springs unseen!

XXVI

Ah, make the most of what we yet may spend,
Before we too into the Dust descend;
   Dust into Dust, and under Dust, to lie,
Sans Wine, sans Song, sans Singer, and — sans End!

XXVII

Alike for those who for To-DAY prepare,
And those that after some To-MORROW stare,
   A Muezzín from the Tower of Darkness cries,
"Fools! your Reward is neither Here nor There!"

XXVIII

Another Voice, when I am sleeping, cries,
"The Flower should open with the Morning skies."
　　And a retreating Whisper, as I wake—
"The Flower that once has blown for ever dies."

XXIX

Why, all the Saints and Sages who discuss'd
Of the Two Worlds so learnedly, are thrust
　　Like foolish Prophets forth; their Words to
　　　　Scorn
Are scatter'd, and their Mouths are stopt with
　　Dust.

XXX

Myself when young did eagerly frequent
Doctor and Saint, and heard great argument
　　About it and about: but evermore
Came out by the same door as in I went.

XXXI

With them the seed of Wisdom did I sow,
And with mine own hand wrought to make it grow:
　　And this was all the Harvest that I reap'd—
"I came like Water, and like Wind I go."

XXXII

Into this Universe, and *Why* not knowing,
Nor *Whence*, like Water willy-nilly flowing:
   And out of it, as Wind along the Waste,
I know not *Whither*, willy-nilly blowing.

XXXIII

What, without asking, hither hurried *Whence?*
And, without asking, *Whither* hurried hence!
   Ah, contrite Heav'n endowed us with the Vine
To drug the memory of that insolence!

XXXIV

Up from Earth's Centre through the Seventh Gate
I rose, and on the Throne of Saturn sate,
   And many Knots unravel'd by the Road;
But not the Master-Knot of Human Fate.

XXXV

There was the Door to which I found no Key:
There was the Veil through which I could not see:
   Some little talk awhile of ME and THEE
There was—and then no more of THEE and ME.

[77]

XXXVI

Earth could not answer; nor the Seas that mourn
In flowing Purple, of their Lord forlorn;
    Nor Heav'n, with those eternal Signs reveal'd
And hidden by the sleeve of Night and Morn.

XXXVII

Then of the THEE IN ME who works behind
The Veil of Universe I cried to find
    A Lamp to guide me through the Darkness; and
Something then said —"An Understanding blind."

XXXVIII

Then to the Lip of this poor earthen Urn
I lean'd, the secret Well of Life to learn:
    And Lip to Lip it murmur'd —"While you live,
"Drink!—for, once dead, you never shall return."

XXXIX

I think the Vessel, that with fugitive
Articulation answer'd, once did live,
    And drink; and that impassive Lip I kiss'd,
How many Kisses might it take—and give!

XL

For I remember stopping by the way
To watch a Potter thumping his wet Clay:
   And with its all-obliterated Tongue
It murmur'd — "Gently, Brother, gently, pray!"

XLI

For has not such a Story from of Old
Down Man's successive generations roll'd
   Of such a clod of saturated Earth
Cast by the Maker into Human mould?

XLII

And not a drop that from our Cups we throw
On the parcht herbage but may steal below
   To quench the fire of Anguish in some Eye
There hidden — far beneath, and long ago.

XLIII

As then the Tulip for her wonted sup
Of Heavenly Vintage lifts her chalice up,
   Do you, twin offspring of the soil, till Heav'n
To Earth invert you like an empty Cup.

XLIV

Do you, within your little hour of Grace,
The waving Cypress in your Arms enlace,
   Before the Mother back into her arms
Fold, and dissolve you in a last embrace.

XLV

And if the Cup you drink, the Lip you press,
End in what All begins and ends in — Yes;
   Imagine then you *are* what heretofore
You *were* — hereafter you shall not be less.

XLVI

So when at last the Angel of the darker drink
Of Darkness finds you by the river-brink,
   And, proffering his Cup, invites your Soul
Forth to your Lips to quaff it — do not shrink.

XLVII

And fear not lest Existence closing *your*
Account, should lose, or know the type no more;
   The Eternal Sáki from that Bowl has pour'd
Millions of Bubbles like us, and will pour.

XLVIII

When You and I behind the Veil are past,
Oh but the long long while the World shall last,
   Which of our Coming and Departure heeds
As much as Ocean of a pebble-cast.

XLIX

One Moment in Annihilation's Waste,
One Moment, of the Well of Life to taste—
   The Stars are setting, and the Caravan
Draws to the Dawn of Nothing—Oh make haste!

L

Would you that spangle of Existence spend
About THE SECRET—quick about it, Friend!
   A Hair, they say, divides the False and True—
And upon what, prithee, does Life depend?

LI

A Hair, they say, divides the False and True;
Yes; and a single Alif were the clue,
   Could you but find it, to the Treasure-house,
And peradventure to THE MASTER too;

L I I

Whose secret Presence, through Creation's veins
Running, Quicksilver-like eludes your pains:
    Taking all shapes from Máh to Máhi; and
They change and perish all—but He remains;

L I I I

A moment guess'd—then back behind the Fold
Immerst of Darkness round the Drama roll'd
    Which, for the Pastime of Eternity,
He doth Himself contrive, enact, behold.

L I V

But if in vain, down on the stubborn floor
Of Earth, and up to Heav'n's unopening Door,
    You gaze To-day, while You are You—how
      then
To-morrow, You when shall be You no more?

L V

Oh, plagued no more with Human or Divine,
To-morrow's tangle to itself resign,
    And lose your fingers in the tresses of
The Cypress-slender Minister of Wine.

L V I

Waste not your Hour, nor in the vain pursuit
Of This and That endeavour and dispute;
　　Better be merry with the fruitful Grape
Than sadden after none, or bitter, Fruit.

L V I I

You know, my Friends, how bravely in my House
For a new Marriage I did make Carouse:
　　Divorced old barren Reason from my Bed,
And took the Daughter of the Vine to Spouse.

L V I I I

For "Is" and "Is-NOT" though with Rule and Line,
And "UP-AND-DOWN" by Logic I define,
　　Of all that one should care to fathom, I
Was never deep in anything but — Wine.

L I X

Ah, but my Computations, People say,
Have squared the Year to human compass, eh?
　　If so, by striking from the Calendar
Unborn To-morrow, and dead Yesterday.

LX

And lately, by the Tavern Door agape,
Came shining through the Dusk an Angel Shape
 Bearing a Vessel on his Shoulder; and
He bid me taste of it; and 't was—the Grape!

LXI

The Grape that can with Logic absolute
The Two-and-Seventy jarring Sects confute:
 The sovereign Alchemist that in a trice
Life's leaden metal into Gold transmute:

LXII

The mighty Mahmúd, Allah-breathing Lord,
That all the misbelieving and black Horde
 Of Fears and Sorrows that infest the Soul
Scatters before him with his whirlwind Sword.

LXIII

Why, be this Juice the growth of God, who dare
Blaspheme the twisted tendril as a Snare?
 A Blessing, we should use it, should we not?
And if a Curse—why, then, Who set it there?

LXIV

I must abjure the Balm of Life, I must,
Scared by some After-reckoning ta'en on trust,
  Or lured with Hope of some Diviner Drink,
When the frail Cup is crumbled into Dust!

LXV

If but the Vine and Love-abjuring Band
Are in the Prophet's Paradise to stand,
  Alack, I doubt the Prophet's Paradise
Were empty as the hollow of one's Hand.

LXVI

Oh threats of Hell and Hopes of Paradise!
One thing at least is certain — *This* Life flies:
  One thing is certain and the rest is lies;
The Flower that once is blown for ever dies.

LXVII

Strange, is it not? that of the myriads who
Before us pass'd the door of Darkness through
  Not one returns to tell us of the Road,
Which to discover we must travel too.

[85]

LXVIII

The Revelations of Devout and Learn'd
Who rose before us, and as Prophets burn'd,
   Are all but Stories, which, awoke from Sleep
They told their fellows, and to Sleep return'd.

LXIX

Why, if the Soul can fling the Dust aside,
And naked on the Air of Heaven ride,
   Is't not a shame — is't not a shame for him
So long in this Clay suburb to abide?

LXX

But that is but a Tent wherein may rest
A Sultan to the realm of Death addrest;
   The Sultan rises, and the dark Ferrásh
Strikes, and prepares it for another guest.

LXXI

I sent my Soul through the Invisible,
Some letter of that After-life to spell:
   And after many days my Soul return'd
And said, " Behold, Myself am Heav'n and Hell : "

LXXII

Heav'n but the Vision of fulfill'd Desire,
And Hell the Shadow of a Soul on fire,
  Cast on the Darkness into which Ourselves,
So late emerg'd from, shall so soon expire.

LXXIII

We are no other than a moving row
Of visionary Shapes that come and go
  Round with this Sun-illumin'd Lantern held
In Midnight by the Master of the Show;

LXXIV

Impotent Pieces of the Game He plays
Upon this Chequer-board of Nights and Days;
  Hither and thither moves, and checks, and slays;
And one by one back in the Closet lays.

LXXV

The Ball no Question makes of Ayes and Noes,
But Right or Left as strikes the Player goes;
  And He that toss'd you down into the Field,
He knows about it all — HE knows — HE knows!

LXXVI

The Moving Finger writes; and, having writ,
Moves on : nor all your Piety nor Wit
　　Shall lure it back to cancel half a Line,
Nor all your Tears wash out a Word of it.

LXXVII

For let Philosopher and Doctor preach
Of what they will, and what they will not—each
　　Is but one Link in an eternal Chain
That none can slip, nor break, nor over-reach.

LXXVIII

And that inverted Bowl we call The Sky,
Whereunder crawling coop'd we live and die,
　　Lift not your hands to *It* for help—for It
As impotently rolls as you or I.

LXXIX

With Earth's first Clay They did the Last Man
　　knead,
And there of the Last Harvest sow'd the Seed;
　　And the first Morning of Creation wrote
What the Last Dawn of Reckoning shall read.

LXXX

Yesterday *This* Day's Madness did prepare;
To-morrow's Silence, Triumph, or Despair:
   Drink! for you know not whence you came,
     nor why:
Drink! for you know not why you go, nor where.

LXXXI

I tell you this—When, started from the Goal,
Over the flaming shoulders of the Foal
   Of Heav'n Parwín and Mushtari they flung,
In my predestin'd Plot of Dust and Soul

LXXXII

The Vine had struck a fibre: which about
If clings my Being—let the Dervish flout;
   Of my Base metal may be filed a Key,
That shall unlock the Door he howls without.

LXXXIII

And this I know: whether the one True Light,
Kindle to Love, or Wrath-consume me quite,
   One Flash of It within the Tavern caught
Better than in the Temple lost outright.

LXXXIV

What! out of senseless Nothing to provoke
A conscious Something to resent the yoke
  Of unpermitted Pleasure, under pain
Of Everlasting Penalties, if broke!

LXXXV

What! from his helpless Creature be repaid
Pure Gold for what he lent us dross-allay'd—
  Sue for a Debt we never did contract,
And cannot answer—Oh the sorry trade!

LXXXVI

Nay, but, for terror of his wrathful Face,
I swear I will not call Injustice grace;
  Not one Good Fellow of the Tavern but
Would kick so poor a Coward from the place.

LXXXVII

Oh Thou, who didst with pitfall and with gin
Beset the Road I was to wander in,
  Thou wilt not with Predestin'd Evil round
Enmesh, and then impute my Fall to Sin?

LXXXVIII

Oh Thou, who Man of baser Earth didst make,
And ev'n with Paradise devise the Snake :
   For all the Sin the Face of wretched Man
Is black with — Man's Forgiveness give — and take.

*   *   *   *   *   *   *

LXXXIX

As under cover of departing Day
Slunk hunger-stricken Ramazán away,
   Once more within the Potter's house alone
I stood, surrounded by the Shapes of Clay.

XC

And once again there gather'd a scarce heard
Whisper among them ; as it were, the stirr'd
   Ashes of some all but extinguisht Tongue,
Which mine ear kindled into living Word.

XCI

Said one among them — "Surely not in vain,
"My Substance from the common Earth was ta'en,
  "That He who subtly wrought me into Shape
"Should stamp me back to shapeless Earth again?"

XCII

Another said, "Why, ne'er a peevish Boy
"Would break the Cup from which he drank in
      Joy;
  "Shall He that of his own free Fancy made
"The Vessel, in an after-rage destroy!"

XCIII

None answer'd this; but after silence spake
Some Vessel of a more ungainly Make;
  "They sneer at me for leaning all awry;
"What! did the Hand then of the Potter shake?"

XCIV

Thus with the Dead as with the Living, *What?*
And *Why?* so ready, but the *Wherefor* not,
  One on a sudden peevishly exclaim'd,
"Which is the Potter, pray, and which the Pot?"

XCV

Said one—"Folks of a surly Master tell,
"And daub his Visage with the Smoke of Hell;
  "They talk of some sharp Trial of us—Pish!
"He's a good Fellow, and 't will all be well."

XCVI

"Well," said another, "Whoso will, let try,
"My Clay with long Oblivion is gone dry:
  "But, fill me with the old familiar Juice,
"Methinks I might recover by-and-bye."

XCVII

So while the Vessels one by one were speaking,
One spied the little Crescent all were seeking:
  And then they jogg'd each other, "Brother!
  Brother!
"Now for the Porter's shoulder-knot a-creaking!"

*   *   *   *   *   *   *

XCVIII

Ah, with the Grape my fading Life provide,
And wash the Body whence the Life has died,
     And lay me, shrouded in the living Leaf,
By some not unfrequented Garden-side.

XCIX

Whither resorting from the vernal Heat
Shall Old Acquaintance Old Acquaintance greet,
     Under the Branch that leans above the Wall
To shed his Blossom over head and feet.

C

Then ev'n my buried Ashes such a snare
Of Vintage shall fling up into the Air,
     As not a True-believer passing by
But shall be overtaken unaware.

CI

Indeed the Idols I have loved so long
Have done my credit in Men's eye much wrong:
     Have drown'd my Glory in a shallow Cup,
And sold my Reputation for a Song.

CII

Indeed, indeed, Repentance oft before
I swore—but was I sober when I swore?   [hand
   And then and then came Spring, and Rose-in-
My thread-bare Penitence apieces tore.

CIII

And much as Wine has play'd the Infidel,
And robb'd me of my Robe of Honour—Well,
   I often wonder what the Vintners buy
One half so precious as the ware they sell.

CIV

Yet Ah, that Spring should vanish with the Rose!
That Youth's sweet-scented manuscript should
      close!
   The Nightingale that in the branches sang,
Ah whence, and whither flown again, who knows!

CV

Would but the Desert of the Fountain yield
One glimpse—if dimly, yet indeed, reveal'd,
   Toward which the fainting Traveller might
      spring,
As springs the trampled herbage of the field!

[95]

CVI

Oh if the World were but to re-create,
That we might catch ere closed the Book of Fate,
   And make The Writer on a fairer leaf
Inscribe our names, or quite obliterate!

CVII

Better, oh better, cancel from the Scroll
Of Universe one luckless Human Soul,
   Than drop by drop enlarge the Flood that rolls
Hoarser with Anguish as the Ages roll.

CVIII

Ah Love! could you and I with Fate conspire
To grasp this sorry Scheme of Things entire,
   Would not we shatter it to bits—and then
Re-mould it nearer to the Heart's Desire!

CIX

But see! The rising Moon of Heav'n again
Looks for us, Sweet-heart, through the quivering
     Plane:
   How oft hereafter rising will she look
Among those leaves—for one of us in vain!

[96]

CX

And when Yourself with silver Foot shall pass
Among the Guests Star-scatter'd on the Grass,
 And in your joyous errand reach the spot
Where I made One — turn down an empty Glass!

*TAMÁM**

**The End.*

RUBÁIYÁT OF
OMAR KHAYYÁM
OF NAISHÁPÚR

THIRD EDITION 1872
FOURTH EDITION 1879
FIFTH EDITION 1889

RUBÁIYÁT of OMAR KHAYYÁM OF NAISHÁPÚR

❦

THIRD EDITION, 1872, FOURTH EDITION, 1879, AND FIFTH EDITION, 1889

I

WAKE! For the Sun, who scatter'd into
flight   [of Night,*
The Stars before him from the Field
Drives Night along with them from Heav'n,
and strikes
The Sultán's Turret with a Shaft of Light.

II

Before the phantom of False morning died,
Methought a Voice within the Tavern cried,
  "When all the Temple is prepared within,
"Why nods the drowsy Worshipper outside?"

In the first draught of the third edition the first and second lines stood thus:

Wake! For the Sun before him into Night
A Signal flung that put the Stars to flight

[101]

III

And, as the Cock crew, those who stood before
The Tavern shouted — "Open then the Door!
  "You know how little while we have to stay,
"And, once departed, may return no more."

IV

Now the New Year reviving old Desires,
The thoughtful Soul to Solitude retires,
  Where the WHITE HAND OF MOSES on the Bough
Puts out, and Jesus from the Ground suspires.

V

Iram indeed is gone with all his Rose,
And Jamshyd's Sev'n-ring'd Cup where no one
        knows;
  But still a Ruby kindles in the Vine,*
And many a Garden by the Water blows.

In the second and third editions:
    But still a Ruby gushes from the Vine,

VI

And David's Lips are lockt; but in divine
High-piping Pehleví,* with "Wine! Wine! Wine!
  "Red Wine!"—the Nightingale cries to the
    Rose
That sallow cheek of hers† to' incarnadine.

VII

Come, fill the Cup, and in the fire of Spring
Your Winter-garment of Repentance fling:
  The Bird of Time has but a little way
To flutter—and the Bird is on the Wing.

VIII

Whether at Naishápúr or Babylon,
Whether the Cup with sweet or bitter run,
  The Wine of Life keeps oozing drop by drop,
The Leaves of Life keep falling one by one.

---

* *In third edition:* **Péhlevi,**

† *In third and fourth editions:* **her's**

IX

Each Morn a thousand Roses brings, you say:
Yes, but where leaves the Rose of Yesterday?
    And this first Summer month that brings the
      Rose
Shall take Jamshyd and Kaikobád away.

X

Well, let it take them! What have we to do
With Kaikobád the Great, or Kaikhosrú?
    Let Zál and Rustum bluster as they will,*
Or Hátim call to Supper—heed not you.

XI

With me along the strip of Herbage strown
That just divides the desert from the sown,
    Where name of Slave and Sultán is forgot—
And Peace to Mahmúd on his golden Throne!

In the third edition:
    Let Zál and Rustum thunder as they will,

XII

A Book of Verses underneath the Bough,
A Jug of Wine, a Loaf of Bread—and Thou
   Beside me singing in the Wilderness—
Oh, Wilderness were Paradise enow!

XIII

Some for the Glories of This World; and some
Sigh for the Prophet's Paradise to come;
   Ah, take the Cash, and let the Credit go,
Nor heed the rumble of a distant Drum!

XIV

Look to the blowing Rose about us—"Lo,*
"Laughing," she says, "into the world I blow,
   "At once the silken tassel of my Purse
"Tear, and its Treasure on the Garden throw."

XV

And those who husbanded the Golden grain,
And those who flung it to the winds like Rain,
   Alike to no such aureate Earth are turn'd
As, buried once, Men want dug up again.

---

* *In the third edition:* Lo,

XVI

The Worldly Hope men set their Hearts upon
Turns Ashes—or it prospers; and anon,
   Like Snow upon the Desert's dusty Face,
Lighting a little hour or two—is gone.*

XVII

Think, in this batter'd Caravanserai
Whose Portals are alternate Night and Day,
   How Sultán after Sultán with his Pomp
Abode his destined † Hour, and went his way.

XVIII

They say the Lion and the Lizard keep
The Courts where Jamshyd gloried and drank deep:
   And Bahrám, that great Hunter—the Wild Ass
Stamps o'er his Head, but cannot break his Sleep.

XIX

I sometimes think that never blows so red
The Rose as where some buried Cæsar bled;
   That every Hyacinth the Garden wears
Dropt in her Lap from some once lovely Head.

---

* *In the two-volume edition of* 1887 : was gone.
† *In the edition of* 1887 : destin'd

X X

And this reviving Herb whose tender Green
Fledges the River-Lip on which we lean —
   Ah, lean upon it lightly! for who knows
From what once lovely Lip it springs unseen!

X X I

Ah, my Belovéd, fill the Cup that clears
To-day of past Regrets* and future Fears:
   To-morrow! — Why, To-morrow I may be
Myself with Yesterday's Sev'n thousand Years.

X X I I

For some we loved, the loveliest and the best
That from his Vintage rolling Time hath prest,†
   Have drunk their Cup a Round or two before,
And one by one crept silently to rest.

---

* *In the edition of* 1887 : Regret

† *In the second and third editions :*
   That from his Vintage rolling Time has prest,

XXIII

And we, that now make merry in the Room
They left, and Summer dresses in new bloom,
   Ourselves must we beneath the Couch of Earth
Descend — ourselves to make a Couch — for whom?

XXIV

Ah, make the most of what we yet may spend,
Before we too into the Dust descend;
   Dust into Dust, and under Dust to* lie,
Sans Wine, sans Song, sans Singer, and — sans
     End!

XXV

Alike for those who for To-DAY prepare,
And those that after some To-MORROW stare,
   A Muezzín from the Tower of Darkness cries,
"Fools! your Reward is neither Here nor There."

---

* *In the edition of* 1887 : Dust, to

XXVI

Why, all the Saints and Sages who discuss'd
Of the Two* Worlds so wisely — they are thrust †
   Like foolish Prophets forth ; their Words to Scorn
Are scatter'd, and their Mouths are stopt with Dust.

XXVII

Myself when young did eagerly frequent
Doctor and Saint, and heard great argument
   About it and about : but evermore
Came out by the same door where in I went.

XXVIII

With them the seed of Wisdom did I sow,
And with mine own hand wrought to make it
     grow ; ‡
   And this was all the Harvest that I reap'd —
"I came like Water, and like Wind I go."

---

* *In the edition of* 1887 : two

† *In the second and third editions :*
    Of the Two Worlds so learnedly, are thrust

‡ *In the second and third editions :*
    And with my own hand wrought to make it grow :

RUBÁIYÁT

XXIX

Into this Universe, and *Why* not knowing
Nor *Whence,* like Water willy-nilly flowing;
   And out of it, as Wind along the Waste,
I know not *Whither,* willy-nilly blowing.

XXX

What, without asking, hither hurried *Whence?*
And, without asking, *Whither* hurried hence!
   Oh, many a Cup of this forbidden Wine
Must drown the memory of that insolence!

XXXI

Up from Earth's Centre through the Seventh Gate
I rose, and on the Throne of Saturn sate,
   And many a Knot unravel'd by the Road;
But not the Master-knot of Human Fate.

XXXII

There was the Door to which I found no Key;
There was the Veil through which I might not see:*
   Some little talk awhile of ME and THEE
There was—and then no more of THEE and ME.

* *In the second and third editions:*
  There was the Veil through which I could not see:

XXXIII

Earth could not answer; nor the Seas that mourn
In flowing Purple, of their Lord forlorn;
   Nor rolling Heaven, with all his Signs reveal'd
And hidden by the sleeve of Night and Morn.

XXXIV

Then of the THEE IN ME who works behind
The Veil, I lifted up my hands to find
   A lamp amid the Darkness; and I heard,
As from Without—"THE ME WITHIN THEE
   BLIND!"

XXXV

Then to the Lip of this poor earthen Urn
I lean'd, the Secret of my Life to learn:
   And Lip to Lip it murmur'd—"While you live,
"Drink!—for, once dead, you never shall return."

XXXVI

I think the Vessel, that with fugitive
Articulation answer'd, once did live,
   And drink; and Ah! the passive Lip I kiss'd,
How many Kisses might it take—and give!

XXXVII

For I remember stopping by the way
To watch a Potter thumping his wet Clay :*
    And with its all-obliterated Tongue
It murmur'd — "Gently, Brother, gently, pray!"

XXXVIII

And has not such a Story from of Old
Down Man's successive generations roll'd
    Of such a clod of saturated Earth
Cast by the Maker into Human mould?†

XXXIX

And not a drop that from our Cups we throw
For Earth to drink of, but may steal below
    To quench the fire of Anguish in some Eye
There hidden — far beneath, and long ago.

---

* *In the third edition:* wet Clay,
† *In the first draught of the third edition the stanza appeared thus :*

    For, in your Ear a moment — of the same
    Poor Earth from which that Human Whisper came,
        The luckless Mould in which Mankind was cast
    They did compose, and call'd him by the name.

In the third edition the first line was altered to :

    Listen — a moment listen ! — Of the same &c.

X L

As then the Tulip for her morning sup
Of Heav'nly Vintage from the soil looks up,*
   Do you devoutly do the like, till Heav'n
To Earth invert you — like an empty Cup.

X L I

Perplext no more with Human or Divine,
To-morrow's tangle to the winds resign,†
   And lose your fingers in the tresses of
The Cypress-slender Minister of Wine.

---

* In the first draught of the third edition the stanza is the same as in the third, fourth and fifth editions, except that the second line is :

    Of Wine from Heav'n her little Tass lifts up,
In the last line of this stanza there is no dash in the fourth edition.

† In the second edition and the first draught of the third edition :

    Oh, plagued no more with Human or Divine
    To-morrow's tangle to itself resign,

XLII

And if the Wine you drink, the Lip you press,*
End in what All begins and ends in — Yes;
    Think then you are To-day what YESTERDAY
You were — To-morrow you shall not be less.

XLIII

So when that Angel of the darker Drink
At last shall find you by the river-brink,
    And, offering his Cup, invite your Soul
Forth to your Lips to quaff — you shall not shrink.†

The first draught of the third edition agrees with the third, fourth and fifth editions except that the first line is:

And if the Cup, and if the Lip you press,

† *In the first draught of the third edition the only change made was from* proffering *to* offering, *but in the third edition the stanza assumed the form in which it also appeared in the fourth edition. The change from* the Angel *to* that Angel *was made in MS. by FitzGerald in a copy of the fourth edition.*

XLIV

Why, if the Soul can fling the Dust aside,
And naked on the Air of Heaven ride,
   Were 't* not a Shame — were 't* not a Shame
     for him
In this clay carcase crippled to abide?

XLV

'T is but a Tent where takes his one day's rest
A Sultán† to the realm of Death addrest;
   The Sultán† rises, and the dark Ferrásh
Strikes, and prepares it for another Guest.

XLVI

And fear not lest Existence closing your
Account, and mine, should know the like no more;
   The Eternal Sákí from that Bowl has pour'd
Millions of Bubbles like us, and will pour.

---

* *In the edition of* 1887 : wer't

† *In the third edition:* Sultan

XLVII

When You and I behind the Veil are past,
Oh, but the long, long while the World shall last,
    Which of our Coming and Departure heeds
As the Sea's self should heed a pebble-cast.*

XLVIII

A Moment's Halt—a momentary taste
Of BEING from the Well amid the Waste—
    And Lo!—the phantom Caravan has reach'd†
The NOTHING it set out from—Oh, make haste!

XLIX

Would you that spangle of Existence spend
About THE SECRET—quick about it, Friend!
    A Hair perhaps divides the False and True—‡
And upon what, prithee, may§ life depend?

---

* *In the third edition:*
    As the SEV'N SEAS should heed a pebble-cast.

† *In the first draught of the third edition:*
    Before the starting Caravan has reach'd
The fourth edition and the edition of 1887 *have:* reacht

‡ *In the edition of* 1887 *there is no dash.*

§ *In the edition of* 1887 : does

L

A Hair perhaps divides the False and True;
Yes; and a single Alif were the clue—
   Could you but find it—to the Treasure-house,
And peradventure to THE MASTER too;

L I

Whose secret Presence, through Creation's veins
Running Quicksilver-like eludes your pains;
   Taking all shapes from Máh to Máhi; and
They change and perish all—but He remains;

L I I

A moment guess'd—then back behind the Fold
Immerst of Darkness round the Drama roll'd
   Which, for the Pastime of Eternity,
He doth* Himself contrive, enact, behold.

---

* *In the second and third editions:* does

LIII

But if in vain, down on the stubborn floor
Of Earth, and up to Heav'n's unopening Door,
   You gaze To-DAY, while You are You—how
     then
To-MORROW, when You shall be You no more?*

LIV

Waste not your Hour, nor in the vain pursuit
Of This and That endeavour and dispute;
   Better be jocund with the fruitful Grape
Than sadden after none, or bitter, Fruit.

LV

You know, my Friends, with what a brave Carouse
I made a Second Marriage in my house;
   Divorced old barren Reason from my Bed,
And took the Daughter of the Vine to Spouse.

---

* *In the first draught of the third edition:*
    To-morrow, when You shall be You no more?

LVI

For "Is" and "Is-not" though with Rule and
    Line*
And "Up-and-down" by Logic I define,†
  Of all that one should care to fathom, I
Was never deep in anything but — Wine.

LVII

Ah, but my Computations, People say,
Reduced the Year to better reckoning? — Nay,
  'Twas only striking from the Calendar
Unborn To-morrow and dead Yesterday.

LVIII

And lately, by the Tavern Door agape,
Came shining through the Dusk an Angel Shape
  Bearing a Vessel on his Shoulder; and
He bid me taste of it; and 'twas — the Grape!

---

* *In the edition of* 1887 : Line,

† *In the third edition:* define

LIX

The Grape that can with Logic absolute
The Two-and-Seventy jarring Sects confute:
    The sovereign Alchemist that in a trice
Life's leaden metal into Gold transmute:

LX

The mighty Mahmúd, Allah-breathing Lord,
That all the misbelieving and black Horde
    Of Fears and Sorrows that infest the Soul
Scatters before him with his whirlwind Sword.

LXI

Why, be this Juice the growth of God, who dare
Blaspheme the twisted tendril as a Snare?
    A Blessing, we should use it, should we not?
And if a Curse — why, then, who set it there?

LXII

I must abjure the Balm of Life, I must,
Scared by some After-reckoning ta'en on trust,
    Or lured with Hope of some Diviner Drink,
To fill the Cup — when crumbled into Dust!

LXIII

Oh threats of Hell and Hopes of Paradise!
One thing at least is certain — *This* Life flies;
   One thing is certain and the rest is Lies;
The Flower that once has blown for ever dies.

LXIV

Strange, is it not? that of the myriads who
Before us pass'd the door of Darkness through,
   Not one returns to tell us of the Road,
Which to discover we must travel too.

LXV

The Revelations of Devout and Learn'd
Who rose before us, and as Prophets burn'd,
   Are all but Stories, which, awoke from Sleep
They told their comrades, and to Sleep return'd.*

LXVI

I sent my Soul through the Invisible,
Some Letter of that After-life to spell:
   And by and by my Soul return'd to me,
And answer'd "I Myself am Heav'n and Hell:"

---

* *In the second and third editions:*
   They told their fellows, and to Sleep return'd.

LXVII

Heav'n but the Vision of fulfill'd Desire,
And Hell the Shadow from a Soul on fire,*
   Cast on the Darkness into which Ourselves,
So late emerged from, shall so soon expire.

LXVIII

We are no other than a moving row
Of Magic Shadow-shapes that come and go
   Round with the Sun-illumined† Lantern held
In Midnight by the Master of the Show;

LXIX

But helpless Pieces of the Game He plays
Upon this Chequer-board of Nights and Days;‡
   Hither and thither moves, and checks, and slays,
And one by one back in the Closet lays.

---

* *In the edition of* 1887 : fire ; *in last line* : emerg'd from,

† *In the edition of* 1887 : Sun-illumin'd

‡ *In the edition of* 1887 : Days :

LXX

The Ball no question makes of Ayes and Noes,
But Here or There as strikes the Player goes;
   And He that toss'd you down into the Field,
He knows about it all—HE knows—HE knows!

LXXI

The Moving Finger writes; and, having writ,
Moves on: nor all your Piety nor* Wit
   Shall lure it back to cancel half a Line,
Nor all your Tears wash out a Word of it.

LXXII

And that inverted Bowl they† call the Sky,
Whereunder crawling coop'd we live and die,
   Lift not your hands to *It* for help—for It
As impotently moves‡ as you or I.

---

* *In the third edition:* and

† *In the second edition and the first draught of the third edition:* we

‡ *In the second and third editions:* rolls

LXXIII

With Earth's first Clay They did the Last Man
  knead,
And there of the Last Harvest sow'd the Seed:
  And the first Morning of Creation wrote
What the Last Dawn of Reckoning shall read.

LXXIV

YESTERDAY *This* Day's Madness did prepare;
TOMORROW'S Silence, Triumph, or Despair:
  Drink! for you know not whence you came, nor
    why:
Drink! for you know not why you go, nor where.

LXXV

I tell you this—When, started from the Goal,
Over the flaming shoulders of the Foal
  Of Heav'n Parwín and Mushtarí* they flung,
In my predestined † Plot of Dust and Soul ‡

---

* *In the third edition:* Mushtari

† *In the edition of* 1887 : predestin'd

‡ *In the third edition:* Soul.

LXXVI

The Vine had struck a fibre : which about
If clings my Being—let the Dervish flout ;
   Of my Base metal may be filed a Key
That shall unlock the Door he howls without.

LXXVII

And this I know : whether the one True Light
Kindle to Love, or Wrath-consume me quite,
   One Flash of It within the Tavern caught
Better than in the Temple lost outright.

LXXVIII

What ! out of senseless Nothing to provoke
A conscious Something to resent the yoke
   Of unpermitted Pleasure, under pain
Of Everlasting Penalties, if broke !

LXXIX

What ! from his helpless Creature be repaid
Pure Gold for what he lent him dross-allay'd—
   Sue for a Debt he * never did contract,
And cannot answer—Oh the sorry trade !

---

* *In the edition of* 1887 : we

LXXX

Oh Thou, who didst with pitfall and with gin
Beset the Road I was to wander in,
    Thou wilt not with Predestined * Evil round
Enmesh, and then impute my Fall to Sin!

LXXXI

Oh Thou, who Man of baser Earth didst make,
And ev'n with Paradise devise the Snake:
    For all the Sin wherewith the Face of Man
Is blacken'd — Man's forgiveness give — and take!

* * * * * * *

LXXXII

As under cover of departing Day
Slunk hunger-stricken Ramazán away,
    Once more within the Potter's house alone
I stood, surrounded by the Shapes of Clay.

---

* In the edition of 1887 : Predestin'd

LXXXIII

Shapes of all Sorts and Sizes, great and small,
That stood along the floor and by the wall;
  And some loquacious Vessels were; and some
Listen'd perhaps, but never talk'd at all.

LXXXIV

Said one among them — "Surely not in vain
"My substance of the common Earth was ta'en
  "And to this Figure moulded, to be broke,
"Or trampled back to shapeless Earth again."

LXXXV

Then said a Second — "Ne'er a peevish Boy
"Would break the Bowl from which he drank in
     joy;
  "And He that with his hand the Vessel made
"Will surely not in after Wrath destroy."

LXXXVI

After a momentary silence spake
Some Vessel of a more ungainly Make;*
  "They sneer at me for leaning all awry:
"What! did the Hand then of the Potter shake?"

---

* *In the edition of* 1887 : make ;

LXXXVII

Whereat some one of the loquacious Lot—
I think a Súfi pipkin—waxing hot—
  "All this of Pot and Potter—Tell me, then,
"Who is the Potter, pray, and who the Pot?"*

LXXXVIII

"Why," said another, "Some there are who tell
"Of one who threatens he will toss to Hell
  "The luckless Pots he marr'd in making—Pish!
"He's a Good Fellow, and 't will all be well. "

LXXXIX

"Well," murmur'd one, "Let whoso make or buy,
"My Clay with long Oblivion is gone dry:
  "But fill me with the old familiar Juice,
"Methinks I might recover by and by."

---

* *In the third edition:*
"Who makes—Who sells—Who buys—Who is the Pot?"

X C

So while the Vessels one by one were speaking,
The little Moon look'd in that all were seeking:
   And then they jogg'd each other, "Brother!
     Brother!
"Now for the Porter's shoulder-knot a-creaking!"

*   *   *   *   *   *   *

X C I

Ah, with the Grape my fading life provide,
And wash the Body whence the Life has died,
   And lay me, shrouded in the living Leaf,
By some not unfrequented Garden-side.

X C I I

That ev'n my buried Ashes such a snare
Of Vintage shall fling up into the Air
   As not a True-believer passing by
But shall be overtaken unaware.

XCIII

Indeed the Idols I have loved so long
Have done my credit in this World much wrong:
 Have drown'd my Glory in a shallow Cup,
And sold my Reputation for a Song.

XCIV

Indeed, indeed, Repentance oft before
I swore — but was I sober when I swore?
 And then and then came Spring, and Rose-in-
  hand
My thread-bare Penitence apieces tore.

XCV

And much as Wine has play'd the Infidel,
And robb'd me of my Robe of Honour — Well,
 I wonder often what the Vintners buy
One half so precious as the stuff they sell.

XCVI

Yet Ah, that Spring should vanish with the Rose!
That Youth's sweet-scented manuscript should
  close!
 The Nightingale that in the branches sang,
Ah whence, and whither flown again, who knows!

XCVII

Would but the Desert of the Fountain yield
One glimpse — if dimly, yet indeed, reveal'd,
   To which the fainting Traveller might spring,
As springs the trampled herbage of the field!

XCVIII

Would but some wingéd Angel ere too late
Arrest the yet unfolded Roll of Fate,
   And make the stern Recorder otherwise
Enregister, or quite obliterate!

XCIX

Ah Love! could you and I with Him conspire
To grasp this sorry Scheme of Things entire,
   Would not we shatter it to bits — and then
Re-mould it nearer to the Heart's Desire!

*   *   *   *   *   *   *

C

Yon rising Moon that looks for us again —
How oft hereafter will she wax and wane;
  How oft hereafter rising look for us
Through this same Garden — and for *one* in vain!

CI*

And when like her, oh Sákí, you shall pass
Among the Guests Star-scatter'd on the Grass,
  And in your joyous errand reach the spot
Where I made One — turn down an empty Glass!

TAMAM

---

* In the third edition:
        And when Yourself with silver Foot shall pass
In the first draught of the third edition: 'Foot' *is changed
to* 'Step.'
In the third edition:
        And in your blissful errand reach the spot

NOTES

NOTES

❧

STanza II.) The "*False Dawn*"; *Subhi Kázib*, a transient Light on the Horizon about an hour before the *Subhi sádik*, or True Dawn; a well-known Phenomenon in the East.

(IV.) New Year. Beginning with the Vernal Equinox, it must be remembered; and (howsoever the old Solar Year is practically superseded by the clumsy *Lunar* Year that dates from the Mohammedan Hijra) still commemorated by a Festival that is said to have been appointed by the very Jamshyd whom Omar so often talks of, and whose yearly Calendar he helped to rectify.

"The sudden approach and rapid advance of the Spring," says Mr. Binning,* "are very striking. Before the Snow is well off the Ground, the Trees burst into Blossom, and the Flowers start forth from the Soil. At *Now Rooz* [*their* New Year's Day] the Snow was lying in patches on the Hills

---

* *Two Years' Travel in Persia,* &c. i. 165.

and in the shaded Vallies, while the Fruit-trees in the Gardens were budding beautifully, and green Plants and Flowers springing up on the Plains on every side —

> ' *And on old Hyems' Chin and icy Crown*
> ' *An odorous Chaplet of sweet Summer buds*
> ' *Is, as in mockery, set.*' —

Among the Plants newly appeared I recognised some old Acquaintances I had not seen for many a Year : among these, two varieties of the Thistle —a coarse species of Daisy like the 'Horse-gowan' —red and white Clover —the Dock —the blue Cornflower —and that vulgar Herb the Dandelion rearing its yellow crest on the Banks of the Watercourses." The Nightingale was not yet heard, for the Rose was not yet blown : but an almost identical Blackbird and Woodpecker helped to make up something of a North-country Spring.

"The White Hand of Moses." Exodus iv. 6; where Moses draws forth his Hand —not, according to the Persians, "*leprous as Snow*," —but *white*, as our May-blossom in Spring perhaps. According to them also the Healing Power of Jesus resided in his Breath.

(v.) Iram, planted by King Shaddád, and now sunk somewhere in the Sands of Arabia. Jamshyd's Seven-ring'd Cup was typical of the 7 Heavens, 7 Planets, 7 Seas, &c., and was a *Divining Cup*.

(vɪ.) *Pehlevi*, the old Heroic *Sanskrit* of Persia. Háfiz also speaks of the Nightingale's *Pehlevi*, which did not change with the People's.
I am not sure if the fourth line refers to the Red Rose looking sickly, or to the Yellow Rose that ought to be Red ; Red, White, and Yellow Roses all common in Persia. I think that Southey, in his Common-Place Book, quotes from some Spanish author about the Rose being White till 10 o'clock ; "Rosa Perfecta" at 2 ; and "perfecta incarnada" at 5.

(x.) Rustum, the "Hercules" of Persia, and Zál his Father, whose exploits are among the most celebrated in the Sháhnáma. Hátim Tai, a well-known type of Oriental Generosity.

(xɪɪɪ.) A Drum—beaten outside a Palace.

(xɪv.) That is, the Rose's Golden Centre.

(xvɪɪɪ.) Persepolis : call'd also *Takht-i-Jamshyd*—

THE THRONE OF JAMSHYD, "*King Splendid*," of the mythical *Peshdádian* Dynasty, and supposed (according to the Sháhnáma) to have been founded and built by him. Others refer it to the Work of the Genie King, Ján Ibn Ján — who also built the Pyramids — before the time of Adam.

BAHRÁM GÚR — *Bahram of the Wild Ass* — a Sassanian Sovereign — had also his Seven Castles (like the King of Bohemia!) each of a different Colour : each with a Royal Mistress within ; each of whom tells him a Story, as told in one of the most famous Poems of Persia, written by Amír Khusraw : all these Sevens also figuring (according to Eastern Mysticism) the Seven Heavens ; and perhaps the Book itself that Eighth, into which the mystical Seven transcend, and within which they revolve. The Ruins of Three of those Towers are yet shown by the Peasantry ; as also the Swamp in which Bahrám sunk, like the Master of Ravenswood, while pursuing his *Gúr*.

> *The Palace that to Heav'n his pillars threw,*
> *And Kings the forehead on his threshold drew —*
>   *I saw the solitary Ringdove there,*
> *And "Coo, coo, coo," she cried ; and "Coo, coo, coo."*

This Quatrain Mr. Binning found, among several
of Háfiz and others, inscribed by some stray hand
among the ruins of Persepolis. The Ringdove's ancient *Pehlevi Coo, Coo, Coo,* signifies also in Persian "*Where? Where? Where?*" In Attár's "Bird-
parliament" she is reproved by the Leader of the
Birds for sitting still, and for ever harping on that
one note of lamentation for her lost Yúsuf.

Apropos of Omar's Red Roses in Stanza xix, I am
reminded of an old English Superstition, that our
Anemone Pulsatilla, or purple "Pasque Flower"
(which grows plentifully about the Fleam Dyke,
near Cambridge), grows only where Danish Blood
has been spilt.

(xxi.) A thousand years to each Planet.

(xxxi.) Saturn, Lord of the Seventh Heaven.

(xxxii.) ME-AND-THEE : some dividual Existence
or Personality distinct from the Whole.

(xxxvii.) One of the Persian Poets — Attár, I think
— has a pretty story about this. A thirsty Traveller

dips his hand into a Spring of Water to drink from. By-and-by comes another who draws up and drinks from an earthen Bowl, and then departs, leaving his Bowl behind him. The first Traveller takes it up for another draught; but is surprised to find that the same Water which had tasted sweet from his own hand tastes bitter from the earthen Bowl. But a Voice—from Heaven, I think—tells him the clay from which the Bowl is made was once *Man;* and, into whatever shape renewed, can never lose the bitter flavour of Mortality.

(xxxix.) The custom of throwing a little Wine on the ground before drinking still continues in Persia, and perhaps generally in the East. Mons. Nicolas considers it "un signe de libéralité, et en même temps un avertissement que le buveur doit vider sa coupe jusqu'à la dernière goutte." Is it not more likely an ancient Superstition; a Libation to propitiate Earth, or make her an Accomplice in the illicit Revel? Or, perhaps, to divert the Jealous Eye by some sacrifice of superfluity, as with the Ancients of the West? With Omar we see something more is signified; the precious Liquor is not lost, but sinks into the ground to refresh the dust of some poor Wine-worshipper foregone.

Thus Háfiz, copying Omar in so many ways: "When thou drinkest Wine pour a draught on the ground. Wherefore fear the Sin which brings to another Gain?"

(XLIII.) According to one beautiful Oriental Legend, Azräel accomplishes his mission by holding to the nostril an Apple from the Tree of Life. This and the two following Stanzas would have been withdrawn, as somewhat *de trop*, from the Text, but for advice which I least like to disregard.

(LI.) From Máh to Máhi; from Fish to Moon.

(LVI.) A Jest, of course, at his Studies. A curious mathematical Quatrain of Omar's has been pointed out to me; the more curious because almost exactly parallel'd by some Verses of Doctor Donne's, that are quoted in Izaak Walton's Lives! Here is Omar: "You and I are the image of a pair of compasses; though we have two heads (sc. our *feet*) we have one body; when we have fixed the centre for our circle, we bring our heads (sc. feet) together at the end." Dr. Donne :

If we be two, we two are so
  As stiff twin-compasses are two;
Thy Soul, the fixt foot, makes no show
  To move, but does if the other do.

And though thine in the centre sit,
  Yet when my other far does roam,
Thine leans and hearkens after it,
  And grows erect as mine comes home.

Such thou must be to me, who must
  Like the other foot obliquely run;
Thy firmness makes my circle just,
  And me to end where I begun.

(LIX.) The Seventy-two Religions supposed to divide the World, *including* Islamism, as some think : but others not.

(LX.) Alluding to Sultan Mahmúd's Conquest of India and its dark people.

(LXVIII.) *Fánúsi khiyál*, a Magic-lantern still used in India; the cylindrical Interior being painted with various Figures, and so lightly poised and

[142]

ventilated as to revolve round the lighted Candle within.

(LXX.) A very mysterious Line in the Original

O dánad O dánad O dánad O ———

breaking off something like our Wood-pigeon's Note, which she is said to take up just where she left off.

(LXXV.) Parwín and Mushtarí—The Pleiads and Jupiter.

(LXXXVII.) This Relation of Pot and Potter to Man and his Maker figures far and wide in the Literature of the World, from the time of the Hebrew Prophets to the present; when it may finally take the name of "Pot theism," by which Mr. Carlyle ridiculed Sterling's "Pantheism." *My* Sheikh, whose knowledge flows in from all quarters, writes to me —

"Apropos of old Omar's Pots, did I ever tell you the sentence I found in 'Bishop Pearson on the Creed'? 'Thus are we wholly at the disposal of His will, and our present and future condition framed and ordered by His free, but wise and just, decrees. *Hath not the potter power over the clay, of the same lump to make one vessel unto honour, and another unto dishonour?* (Rom. ix. 21.) And can that earth-artificer have a freer power over his *brother potsherd* (both being made of the same metal), than God hath over him, who, by the strange fecundity of His omnipotent power, first made the clay out of nothing, and then him out of that?'" And again—from a very different quarter—"I had to refer the other day to Aristophanes, and came by chance on a curious Speaking-pot story in the Vespæ, which I had quite forgotten.

Φιλοκλέων.　Ἄκουε, μὴ φεῦγ'·　ἐν Συβάρει γυνή ποτε
　　　　　　　κατέαξ' ἐχῖνον.　　　　　　　　l. 1435
Κατήγορος.　Ταῦτ' ἐγὼ μαρτύρομαι.
Φι.　　　　Οὐχῖνος οὖν ἔχων τιν' ἐπεμαρτύρατο·
　　　　　Εἶθ' ἡ Συβαρῖτις εἶπεν, εἰ ναὶ τὰν κόραν
　　　　　τὴν μαρτυρίαν ταύτην ἐάσας, ἐν τάχει
　　　　　ἐπίδεσμον ἐπρίω, νοῦν ἂν εἶχες πλείονα.

"The Pot calls a bystander to be a witness to his bad treatment. The woman says, 'If, by Proserpine, instead of all this 'testifying' (comp. Cuddie and his mother in 'Old Mortality!') you would buy yourself a rivet, it would show more sense in you!' The Scholiast explains *echinus* as ἄγγος τι ἐκ κεράμου."

One more illustration for the oddity's sake from the "Autobiography of a Cornish Rector," by the late James Hamley Tregenna. 1871.

"There was one old Fellow in our Company — he was so like a Figure in the 'Pilgrim's Progress' that Richard always called him the 'ALLEGORY,' with a long white beard — a rare Appendage in those days — and a Face the colour of which seemed to have been baked in, like the Faces one used to see on Earthenware Jugs. In our Country-dialect Earthenware is called '*Clome*'; so the Boys of the Village used to shout out after him — 'Go back to the Potter, old Clome-face, and get baked over again.' For the 'Allegory,' though shrewd enough in most things, had the reputation of being '*saift-baked*,' i.e., of weak intellect."

(xc.) At the Close of the Fasting Month, Rama-zán (which makes the Musulman unhealthy and unamiable), the first Glimpse of the New Moon (who rules their division of the Year), is looked for with the utmost Anxiety, and hailed with Acclamation. Then it is that the Porter's Knot may be heard—toward the *Cellar*. Omar has elsewhere a pretty Quatrain about the same Moon—

" *Be of Good Cheer—the sullen Month will die,*
" *And a young Moon requite us by and by:*
  " *Look how the Old one meagre, bent, and wan*
" *With Age and Fast, is fainting from the Sky!*"

CHRONOLO-
GICAL TABLE

COMPARATIVE
TABLE, ETC.

O MAR *Khayyám (Ghiyathed-din
ibn el Feth 'UMER ibn Ibráhím
el KHAYYÁMI)*

Born   1018?–1024?–1050?–1060?

Accession of Alp Arslan as Sultan of Persia 1064

*Omar Khayyám granted pension of 1200
gold mithcals ($3,000)*   1070?

Reign of Malik Shah, Sultan of Persia

1072–Nov. 17, 1092

Death of the Vizier Nizám ul Mulk Oct. 15, 1092

*Omar Khayyám employed in revising the
calendar for Malik Shah (the* Tarikh-i-
Jelali *or* Jelalian Era)   1079

Religious war in Nishápúr   1095–1097

Conquest of Asia Minor by the Turks   1084

Death of William the Conqueror   1087

Siege of Antioch   1098

Siege of Jerusalem by Godfrey de Bouillon 1099

Baldwin, King of Jerusalem   1100

*Massacre of the Ismailiyeh of followers of
Hasan ibn Sabbáh*   1101

*Death of Omar Khayyám** 1123–1124
Story of the apparition of Omar told by
Dr. Hyde. One quatrain quoted 1700
Von Hammer-Purgstall's Translation of
25 Quatrains 1818
Birth of Edward FitzGerald March 31, 1809
FitzGerald enters Trinity College, Cambridge 1826
Anonymous Translations of Omar published in Fraser *April,* 1840
FitzGerald begins to study Persian with Professor E. B. Cowell 1853

---

* *Mr. John Payne says that Nizám ul Mulk was of the same age as Omar Khayyám; if then Nizám was born in 1018 there may be some foundation for the statement of A. Houtoum-Schindler that Omar died in 1124 "over a hundred years old." He himself says he had lived a rounded century:* —

That which I am I am, O Lord, by Thy decree;
An hundred years in ease Thy grace hath fostered me;
An hundred more I fain would sin, so I might see
Whether 's the more, my sin or Thine indulgency.

Payne: 681.

Publication of Garcin de Tassy's " Note sur les Rubä'iyat de 'Omar Khaïam " 1857

MS. of FitzGerald's first translation sent to Fraser *January,* 1858

First edition printed *April 27,* 1859

French-Persian Edition of J. B. Nicolas 1867

FitzGerald's second edition 1868

FitzGerala's third edition 1872

Graf von Schack's German translation 1878

First American edition from third London 1878

FitzGerald's fourth edition 1879

F. Bodenstedt's German translation 1881

E. H. Whinfield's first translation 1882

E. H. Whinfield's English-Persian edition 1883

Death of Edward FitzGerald *June* 14, 1883

Elihu Vedder's illustrated edition 1884

Grolier Club edition 1885

Two-Volume Memorial Edition, edited by Michael Kerney 1887

John L. Garner's " Strophes of Omar Khay-yam " 1888

FitzGerald's fifth edition 1889

Justin Huntly McCarthy's prose rendering 1889

Herbert Wilson Greene's Latin version of
    FitzGerald   1893
Mosher's Bibelot Edition   1893
Mosher's Old World Edition   1895
Boston Multivariorum edition (L. C. Page
    and Company)   1895
Mosher's Bibelot reprint of McCarthy   1896
Handy Volume Edition (comparative and
    with Absálám and Absál)   1897
Edward Heron-Allen's reproduction of
    Ouseley MS. and literal prose translation 1898
John Payne's Villon Club edition containing
    metrical translations of 845 Rubá'iyát   1898
John Leslie Garner's "Stanzas" (second
    edition of Strophes)   1898
Comparative edition with Introduction by
    Talcott Williams, Philadelphia   1898
Lark edition, San Francisco   1898
Note edition, San Francisco   1898
Bradley edition, New York   1898
Edward Heron-Allen's second English and
    first American edition (L. C. Page and
    Company)   1898

N. H. Dole's privately printed Breviary
Bilingual Edition, containing the Fitz-
Gerald-Greene versions   *July*, 1898
For complete bibliography see Dole's Multiva-
riorum, and Heron-Allen's " Rubá'iyát "
published by L. C. Page and Company,
Boston.

COMPARATIVE TABLE OF STANZAS IN THE FIVE EDITIONS

First Edition	Second Edition	Third, Fourth, and Fifth Editions
I	I	I
II	II	II
III	III	III
IV	IV	IV
V	V	V
VI	VI	VI
VII	VII	VII
VIII	IX	IX
IX	X	X
X	XI	XI
XI	XII	XII
XII	XIII	XIII
XIII	XV	XIV
XIV	XVII	XVI
XV	XVI	XV
XVI	XVIII	XVII
XVII	XIX	XVIII

COMPARATIVE TABLE

First Edition	Second Edition	Third, Fourth, and Fifth Editions
XVIII	XXIV	XIX
XIX	XXV	XX
XX	XXI	XXI
XXI	XXII	XXII
XXII	XXIII	XXIII
XXIII	XXVI	XXIV
XXIV	XXVII	XXV
XXV	XXIX	XXVI
XXVI	LXVI	LXIII
XXVII	XXX	XXVII
XXVIII	XXXI	XXVIII
XXIX	XXXII	XXIX
XXX	XXXIII	XXX
XXXI	XXXIV	XXXI
XXXII	XXXV	XXXII
XXXIII	XXXVII	XXXIV
XXXIV	XXXVIII	XXXV
XXXV	XXXIX	XXXVI
XXXVI	XL	XXXVII
XXXVII		
XXXVIII	XLIX	XLVIII

COMPARATIVE TABLE

First Edition	Second Edition	Third, Fourth, and Fifth Editions
XXXIX	LVI	LIV
XL	LVII	LV
XLI	LVIII	LVI
XLII	LX	LVIII
XLIII	LXI	LIX
XLIV	LXII	LX
XLV		
XLVI	LXXIII	LXVIII
XLVII	XLV	XLII
XLVIII	XLVI	XLIII
XLIX	LXXIV	LXIX
L	LXXV	LXX
LI	LXXVI	LXXI
LII	LXXVIII	LXXII
LIII	LXXIX	LXXIII
LIV	LXXXI	LXXV
LV	LXXXII	LXXVI
LVI	LXXXIII	LXXVII
LVII	LXXXVII	LXXX
LVIII	LXXXVIII	LXXXI
LIX	LXXXIX	LXXXII

COMPARATIVE TABLE

First Edition	Second Edition	Third, Fourth, and Fifth Editions
LX	XCIV	LXXXVII
LXI	XCI	LXXXIV
LXII	XCII	LXXXV
LXIII	XCIII	LXXXVI
LXIV	XCV	LXXXVIII
LXV	XCVI	LXXXIX
LXVI	XCVII	XC
LXVII	XCVIII	XCI
LXVIII	C	XCII
LXIX	CI	XCIII
LXX	CII	XCIV
LXXI	CIII	XCV
LXXII	CIV	XCVI
LXXIII	CVIII	XCIX
LXXIV	CIX	C
LXXV	CX	CI
	VIII	VIII
	XIV	
	XX	Note on
		XVIII
	XXVIII	

COMPARATIVE TABLE

Second Edition	Third, Fourth, and Fifth Editions
XXXVI	XXXIII
XLI	XXXVIII
XLII	XXXIX
XLIII	XL
XLIV	
XLVII	XLVI
XLVIII	XLVII
L	XLIX
LI	L
LII	LI
LIII	LII
LIV	LIII
LV	XLI
LIX	LVII
LXIII	LXI
LXIV	LXII
LXV	
LXVII	LXIV
LXVIII	LXV
LXIX	XLIV
LXX	XLV

COMPARATIVE TABLE

Second Edition	Third, Fourth, and Fifth Editions
LXXI	LXVI
LXXII	LXVII
LXXVII	
LXXX	LXXIV
LXXXIV	LXXVIII
LXXXV	LXXIX
LXXXVI	
XC	LXXXIII
XCIX	
CV	XCVII
CVI	XCVIII
CVII	

Printed in the United States
30272LVS00002B/149-150